Song
OF
Death

SUPERNATURAL SAVIOR'S SERIES

C.A. VARIAN

TRIGGER WARNINGS

There are mature themes throughout this book, and it is not intended for readers under 17 years of age.

The following themes are explored in Song of Death: Graphic (consensual) sexual content, captivity, slavery, suicide, abduction, torture, vulgar language, and murder.

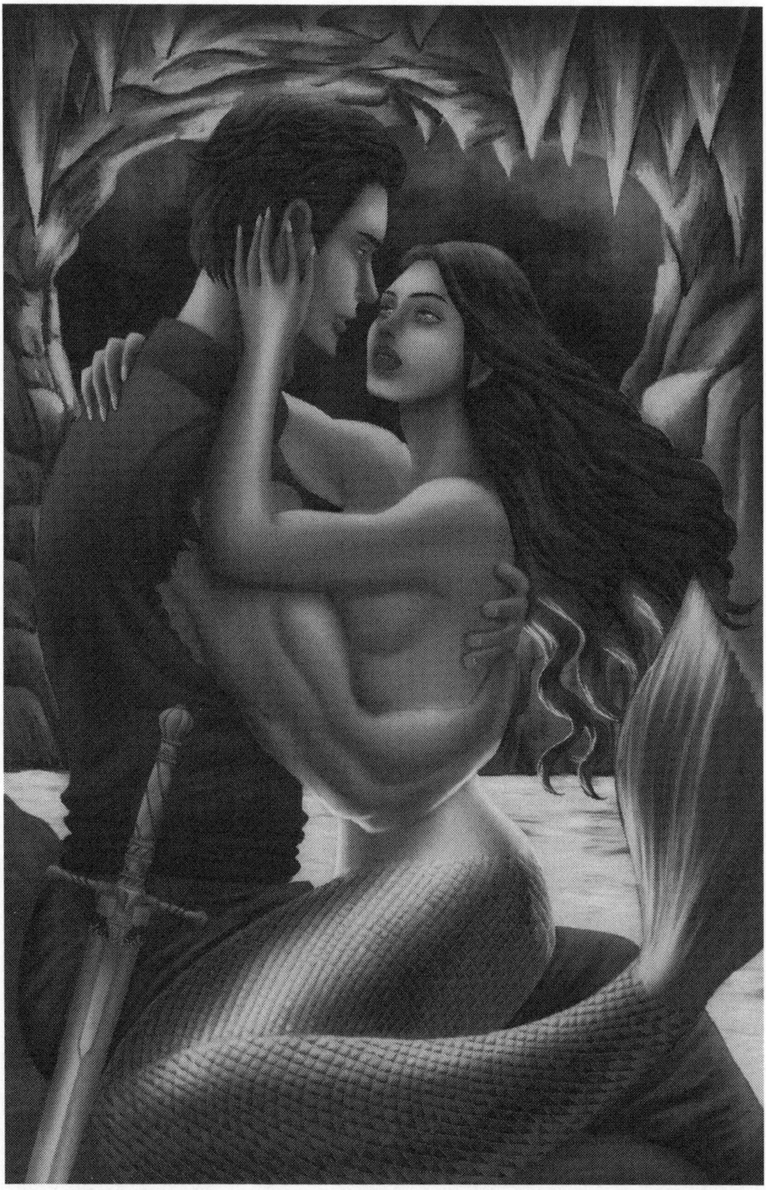

ORORIS

TOWN
CITY
MOUNTAIN PASS

Chapter One
I'll Do Anything

"Help!" Azure Galanides screamed as the current pulled her little sister under the tumultuous waves. "Someone! Please! Save her!"

She had only taken her eyes off the seven-year-old for a moment, but that was enough for Daneliya to drift out of her reach. No one was on the beach. They were on their own.

Running into the rough waters, Azure tried to grasp her sister's hand, but the child only thrashed, before going under the surface once more, pulled further into the current. Sobs poured freely out of Azure, salty tears mixing with the brine of the Lamalis Sea.

"Someone! Please!"

Daneliya did not surface again. Panicked, Azure jumped forward and sucked in a deep breath as she dove under. She searched for a sign of the child, but opening her eyes was useless. The dark waters burned, obscuring her vision. She couldn't see anything.

She flailed her limbs violently, feeling around for her sister in the rough seas, but her hands found nothing. Her lungs protested, forcing her up for air, but a wave crashed over her and almost forced her under once more. She choked and sputtered as the water assaulted her nose and mouth before she could inhale.

Tiny arms drifted toward her with the next crest. Reaching out, she grabbed her sister as she fought the push and pull of the current in a desperate attempt to reach the beach. Storm clouds hovered ominously above, completely blocking out the sun, as she laid her sister's limp body on the sandy shore. The eerie darkness that swallowed up the calm afternoon gave the deserted coast a sinister feeling.

"Daneliya!" Azure sobbed as she shook her sister's body. The adolescent had turned a sickening shade of blue, but she couldn't give up. "Please! Someone! Help us!" She pushed on the child's chest frantically, desperate to expel the water from her little lungs, but it was useless. There was no sign of the color receding, no sign of breath.

A flash of lightning cracked across the darkening sky as Azure wept over her sister's tiny frame. Daneliya was gone. She'd lost her, and it was all her fault. The seven-year-old was her responsibility, and she failed to keep her safe.

At eighteen years old, Azure knew better than to take her eyes off the child for even a moment. With that one mistake, she had killed the last of her family—the only person she had left in this life. She'd already lost her parents, and now Daneliya, too. There was no one left and no more reason for her to carry on.

Looking over her shoulder at the violent waves that took her sister from her, Azure considered meeting the same end. All she had to do was walk in and let go. There was no point in persevering anymore. The air thickened around her, feeling heavy against her skin, as she looked down at Daneliya's lifeless body once more. Once the waves took her, the pain of being the only survivor would disappear. Everything would disappear. The agony that small mistake caused, the feeling of her heart wrenching in two, would end.

The humidity continued to condense until water droplets formed and hung around her, suspended in midair. An icy hand touched her shoulder, jolting her to the side. Azure whipped her head around, but no one was there. Although it was midday, the sky had darkened so much that it looked like night. She shook off her grim thoughts and bent to lift her sister's body, intending to remove her from the beach and bring her somewhere safe, but the invisible hand touched her shoulder again. Freezing in place, Azure sucked in a deep breath before looking up.

Her eyes darted to the side, spotting a hooded figure beside her, its face hidden in shadows. Although she couldn't explain it, power seemed to radiate out from them, encircling her and holding her in place. She couldn't make out the face of the being as it loomed over her like a silent sentinel—an overseeing god with no empathy for its people. *Watching, but not helping.*

"Help her. Please." Azure wept over her sister, defeated and shivering, as her voice came out as a whispered plea. She knew Daneliya was beyond saving, but she still begged for a miracle.

The cloaked individual lowered themselves over the young girl's body, placing a pale hand on the child's still chest. It did not rise and fall. There were no signs of life. She was gone. Azure's breath caught in her throat as she continued to plead.

"Can you help her? Please. I'll do anything."

Silence filled the shoreline in the place of her sister's beating heart. It was enough to make Azure wonder if the being was a figment of her imagination.

"Would you trade yourself?" The hooded figure didn't look at Azure as it spoke, but the voice was feminine. Azure swallowed back the bitter dread the words invoked within her. She understood the question, but still hoped she had misunderstood, almost afraid to answer.

"Trade myself how?"

"Her soul for yours." The voice was icy and devoid of emotion, sending shivers across Azure's body, chilling her blood.

"Yes." Azure's response was only a whisper, but there was no question. *Yes.* She would trade her life for her sister's. Daneliya was too young to die.

Freezing fingers grasped Azure's hand without warning. The figure's grip was crushing as its jagged nails tore into her flesh.

"Stop! You're hurting me!" She whimpered as she struggled to pull her hand away, but it was no use. The hold only tightened further. There was no response as she watched droplets of her crimson blood soak into the golden sand. When the hooded woman let go and returned her hand to Daneliya's chest, Azure cradled her bleeding appendage. She was unsure of what to say or do as she watched her sister's body, silently praying for life to return to her bluish complexion while the mysterious woman muttered unintelligible words to herself.

Time stood still. The only sounds were Azure's thundering heart and the shallow whispers of her breath. She squeezed her eyes closed and forced herself to take a deep breath, exhaling slowly to steady herself, as she silently begged the universe to bring her sister back.

After a few painfully uneventful moments, a forceful gasp escaped Daneliya's mouth, followed by a frantic attempt to suck in air. The world spun around Azure at the miraculous sight, making it difficult to breathe.

"Return to these waters before the sun descends. If you do not, you will not live to see the morning."

The words were cold. Distant. Azure turned to face the dark figure with skeptical questions on her tongue, but before she could speak, the figure disappeared. She wanted to ask who the woman was, wanted to thank her, but there was no trace of her having ever been there, except for the fact that Daneliya was alive.

The sun peeked from behind the clouds, warming her skin with its brilliant rays, as her sister's eyes opened.

"Sissy?" Daneliya's tiny voice was strained and unsure. Crushing the girl against her chest, Azure clung to her little sister as though she were afraid the child would disappear just as her savior had. Tears of joy mingled with the salty water that soaked the little girl's dress. Lifting the shivering child in her arms, Azure headed back toward their home just as the birds began to sing.

"It's okay. Everything will be okay."

CHAPTER TWO
3 YEARS LATER

Azure hissed through her clenched teeth as the burning, torn skin of her back throbbed.

"Hold still. I'm almost done." Ocevia blew on her back as she screwed the lid back on the ointment tin. "They should scab over soon. If you would stop defying her, she would stop having you whipped."

Although she knew Ocevia was right, Azure still rolled her eyes. It was no secret that she couldn't seem to stay out of trouble. Ever since she gave up her life to save her sister's, and was forced into servitude under the sea, she had been in nonstop trouble. The Sea Goddess, Miris, was difficult to please.

"Even if I stayed out of trouble, she would still find a reason to punish me."

"You're probably right." Her friend rinsed her hands in the salty water. Waves crashed violently against their small cove, making it a dangerous place to rest. At least for humans. Mermaids like them, however, spent many daylight hours on the small, rocky islands that dotted the Lamalis Sea. "Are you going to be ready to go back out tonight?"

Azure glanced at the markings she had carved in the rock wall at the back of the cave. One hundred and forty-three carvings stared back at her, and the five thousand she needed never felt so unattainable. She needed to collect five thousand souls to pay her debt to Miris. Then, if the Sea Goddess was to be believed, Azure would be free to return to her human life... if Daneliya even remembered her. She let out a shuddering breath as she gazed back at her friend. "I don't think I have a choice. My back can't take any more lashings just yet."

Ocevia pursed her lips, brushing her long blond hair away from her beautiful, delicate face. She and Azure were the same age, although the blond mermaid looked so much younger.

All the mermaids were stunning. It helped them claim their targets. Their angelic voices and beautiful features made it easy to lure men to their deaths. The humans wrecked their ships in the rough seas and drowned within the waves for a chance to claim a mermaid as their own. Every soul they claimed fed the beasts that were Miris and her henchmen, who held the chains of the mermaids and enforced their life debts.

"You really don't. You'll never be free if you keep putting more marks on your back than on that wall." Ocevia gestured to the back of the cave as she held Azure's stare.

Azure sat up with a grunt, wincing as the wounds on her back stretched with the movement. Her friend was right. She didn't know how many lashes she had taken the day before, since she'd passed out after the first few, but she had definitely taken more lashes than souls over the past three years.

"Yea... that's going to hurt you for a while." The blond mermaid grimaced as Azure moved in slow, careful motions to avoid aggravating the fresh wounds.

"I'm aware. I'm the one who always takes the whip, after all. Have you ever even been punished by Miris?"

Ocevia looked out over the horizon, her gaze vacant as she inhaled. The smell of briny water filled the moist air of the cave, as the sound of waves crashing against the jagged rocks echoed throughout the enclosed space. She remained silent for a long time before she answered Azure's question. "I have not." Ocevia shook her head, the cloudy look in her eye clearing as she continued. "It's a stormy one today. Bad for the sailors, good for us."

Sighing, Azure pulled her top back over her breasts. It was not much more than a strip of seaweed, but there was no place for modesty in her life—not anymore. Everything about her was meant to allure her victims now. "I don't consider it good for me either. I never wanted to be a killer."

Their stares locked, and Ocevia's brilliant turquoise eyes softened at Azure's words. "The water takes lives. We're just bystanders."

Azure let out an incredulous huff as she tucked her onyx hair behind her ear. The wavy locks still felt foreign to her, having taken on a violet sheen in her transformation. Nothing remained the same after becoming a mermaid. As she stared at a puddle that pooled on the cave floor, her reflection taunted her. Turquoise eyes, the same shade as every other mermaid, stared back at her as if to remind her that she was far from the human she'd once been.

Carefully crawling to her feet, she joined her friend at the mouth of the cave. Although they could shift into a human form and use their legs, they were forbidden from entering any lands where humans dwelled. Caves and small, uninhabited islands were where they rested when they left the sea. Some chose to spend their moments of respite in underwater caverns, or in the Sea Goddess' underwater palace, but Azure preferred to stay as far from Miris as she could when given the chance. "That's just wishful thinking, and you know it. Most of those ships would make it safely across if it were not for us. She has turned us into monsters. The water is the weapon, but we are the ones who wield it to claim the victims."

Ocevia sniffed as she turned away, wiping her cheek. "We don't have a choice, Azure. You try to deny our fate, but all it does is get you whipped. It's not getting you any closer to seeing your sister again. Surely you must know this."

The thought of Daneliya growing up without her sent her heart plummeting into her stomach. Azure's voice softened as the emotions ate away at her insides. "I know." She placed her hand on her friend's icy elbow. "Look, I'm sorry. I just hate this."

Wrapping Azure in an embrace, Ocevia silently cried on her friend's shoulder. "I do too. We are all in this together. None of us want to live like this."

Azure snorted. "I can think of a few who might. *The merbitches.*" Oona and Lucia, two mermaids she despised, had fulfilled their life debts long ago but remained in this cursed form, forsaking their human lives. They enjoyed being monsters who played as though they were gods with innocent mortal lives. They were evil and vicious to their very cores.

Ocevia, her only friend, nodded against her shoulder. The blond beauty was not a monster. If anything, she was the kindest among the forsaken merpeople. She'd been paying off her life debt since she was a young girl. If she remembered her life prior to her transformation, she didn't talk about it, but it had not hardened her. She was not defiant like Azure. She followed the rules, and her back was as unblemished as her record. Azure didn't know what her friend had received in exchange for her extensive life debt, but the fact that Ocevia owed fifty thousand

souls to Miris was enough to tell her it was something *big*. Ocevia had never offered an explanation, and Azure wasn't even sure if her friend had any memory of the exchange.

"Come on. Let's get something to eat."

She changed the subject, hoping to distract from the sadness her words had invoked within her friend, as she led the way to the crates that lined the far wall. Azure grabbed a few pieces of the dried fish that made up the bulk of their meals, aside from any fresh fish they ate while in the sea.

Honestly, she was tired of fish. She had never enjoyed eating them before she entered the salty waters as a slave to the wicked, and that didn't change with her transformation. Sometimes, she got to eat fruits and vegetables on one of the small islands that speckled the sea, but it wasn't often enough for her tastes.

Giving Ocevia a handful of the small fish, they sat on the stone platform that served as a bed.

"I could really go for something other than dried fish right now." Ocevia held her nose as she took a bite.

Azure snickered. "Me too. I don't remember my mother's cooking, but my father made a tasty stuffed goose. I could go for either at this moment."

"That sounds delicious. I don't actually remember my mother's cooking either, but I can imagine she was great at it." Her friend's voice became softer, more melancholy. "When I gain my freedom, you must take me to meet your family."

Azure's heart thudded as she thought of her family. "All that's left is my little sister. I hope she found a home with someone who cares for her. With only one hundred and forty-three souls after three years, my sister will be grown and married by the time I'm free. With my luck, she will have moved away, and I'll never be able to find her."

"I'm sorry, Azure. I didn't mean to bring that up. I didn't realize about your parents."

Azure squeezed Ocevia's hand. "No. It's okay. It's my fault for never telling you about them. I've moved past that loss."

"I understand. It's hard to bring up things that cause us pain, especially when we are supposed to be hardened out here."

Her friend could not be more correct. Hardening their hearts was the only way to survive this captivity. If she didn't, watching the life drain from the drowning victims, after witnessing her own sister suffer the same fate, would be enough to break her.

Azure met Ocevia's eyes. "And what about your family? Will I ever be able to meet them?"

No matter how much Azure tried to open the conversation, her friend never spoke about her past.

Sighing, Ocevia fidgeted with the shell necklace that never left her neck. "Maybe someday."

Ocevia's noncommittal response held no hope. Azure didn't know for sure, but something told her she would never be able to meet her friend's family.

T he storm was raging by the time Azure and Ocevia dared to leave their cave. The crashing waves would aid them in sinking ships and claiming souls, but the stormy weather would also limit the number of ships traversing the sea.

Azure didn't know if she was glad for the weather or not. She needed to send souls into the sea to reduce her life debt to Miris, but taking lives weighed heavily on her conscience, and she wasn't even sure if it was worth it. The likelihood of her little sister still living in their old cottage, especially by the time Azure finished paying off her life debt, was minimal. Daneliya would be long gone by the time she ended five thousand innocent lives. Any other thought was just an unrealistic dream.

"Usual spot?" Ocevia shifted forms, her human legs replaced with an iridescent turquoise tail as she dropped to sit on the edge of the rock.

Their usual spot was near the southern shipping channel, closest to the Kingdom of Thatia, Azure's homeland. Although ships could navigate through many parts of the sea, they often stayed near the same stretches of water, because they were deeper than the areas near the coast.

Most of the ships in the channel belonged to merchants that brought goods from the mainland of Thatia to the other coastal kingdoms of Avrearyn, Zourin, and Vidaica. But there were also pirate ships that sought to do harm on those seas. Because the pirates were dangerous nuisances, the mermaids typically aimed to sink those ships first, but merchants were also fair targets.

"Our usual spot works for me."

Sitting next to her friend on the rocks, Azure shifted her legs into her iridescent purple tail and slid into the cold water, disappearing below the surface. Her stomach always sank when they headed for their spot. She constantly fought an internal battle about whether she could escape from her captivity. But she couldn't. The only way to get rid of her tail permanently was to fulfill her obligations to the Sea Goddess. It was either that, or to die. If there was another way, she didn't know of it. So, with Ocevia by her side, and her heart leaden in her stomach, the two set out to claim, albeit begrudgingly, more lives.

The storm was so violent they had to swim below the surface to avoid mouthfuls of salty water. Because of the storm, the water was frigid, although Azure had become more acclimated to the extreme temperatures during her time as a slave. It was the only thing she had gotten used to. Unlike when she was human, her skin no longer shriveled after long stints in the sea, and she was able to dry off much quicker than before. Everything was different now. Even her voice had gotten clearer, and her ability to sing was more fine-tuned. These changes made claiming lives easier, but her conscience could not be overlooked. Her aversion to the task grew with each soul she was forced to steal.

They arrived at their usual hunting grounds an hour later and lifted their heads above the surface, scanning the horizon. There were no boats around at that moment, but they waited for one to show up, anyway. The thunderstorm continued to rage, making it difficult to see very far. Lightning struck in the distance, flashing brilliantly against the darkened sky, and its crackle drove Azure back below the water. The last thing she needed was to get struck by lightning.

"Anyone out on the water tonight is a fool." Azure said as soon as she resurfaced. She waited for a response, knowing that they were just as foolish for braving the electricity-filled sky. Grimacing, Ocevia used her hands and tail to tread water as she continued to search for a target.

"I admit that tonight doesn't seem like it will be very fruitful. The storm is too bad. Let's hang around for a bit, though. A ship could show up."

Azure was not comfortable being out in such a turbulent storm, but she nodded anyway, and joined Ocevia in her search. She wondered if the other mermaids were out hunting, or if they were the only ones dumb enough to chance it.

Just as she pondered if they were alone, the water bubbled from beneath them. It was their only, albeit brief, warning before Oona and Lucia, the sociopathic mermaids who made up Goddess Miris' inner circle, surfaced. Their savage smirks made her blood boil.

"This is our spot," Azure spat at them. "You need to find another location." She never hesitated to mouth off to the duo, even though she knew they were dangerous.

Oona's sick smile widened as her black hair floated like an ink spill around her. "You and your weak little friend do not own any of this water. We hunt where we choose. Go ahead. Try to take souls from us. It won't end well for you."

Azure's pulse quickened, her pounding heartbeat louder in her ears than the roaring thunder overhead. She readied her retort when movement in the distance caught her eye and distracted her. A merchant ship was approaching from the direction of Vidaica. Silence descended on them as they watched it approach, rocking in the violent winds.

Grabbing Ocevia's hand, Azure pulled her toward the vessel and away from their enemies. She could hear their competition behind them, but it didn't matter. Determined to reach the target first, she headed for a rock outcropping that ran along the side of the channel. Once they reached it, Azure swam in place and began to sing. Ocevia joined in, her voice weaving perfectly into the song as they created a sensual, alluring tune. She saw Oona and Lucia across the channel but could barely make out their singing over the storm. Determined to outshine the bloodthirsty duo, Azure sang louder in the hopes of getting the ship's attention first.

Come to me,

your long-lost love,

and hold me in your arms.

The gods above,

and the goddesses below,

brought me back to you.

Chapter Three
A Foolish Wish

The ship veered in their direction, and a shiver of anticipation, mixed with self-loathing, raced through Azure's body. It was time to carry out her cursed duties. She would kill on this night, and she would hate herself for it.

Moving out of the vessel's path, she and Ocevia hid behind a large rock outcropping near the edge of the channel as they continued to sing their haunting song. The craft drifted toward them as though it was merely a ghost ship sailing across the raging waters, before it collided with the rocks before them.

The sound of wood splintering against stone set Azure's teeth on edge. She squeezed her eyes shut and told herself it was the water taking the lives and not her, but she couldn't convince herself. The familiar sound of their victims' screams rang out into the night, highlighted by the booming thunder overhead.

They were the same screams that haunted her dreams and jolted her awake at night. The sheer volume of horrific outcries told her that at least fifty men had been aboard the damned vessel. She and Ocevia would share the souls claimed from this shipwreck, as they always did, but she knew there would be a fight with the bitches across the channel. There was no way Oona would allow them to take credit for all the lost lives, even though it was Azure and Ocevia's song that brought about their downfall.

"I'm going to head for the stern to see how many are already in the water." Ocevia's voice pulled Azure from the depths of her mind. She nodded and fell back into the shadows as her friend swam away. The frantic screams lessened as the sea claimed the goddess' sacrifices. Closing her eyes, she waited for their suffering to end. Her chest grew tighter as each life was snuffed out, the descending silence deafening. Bile burned her throat. She tried to breathe through it, but the burn never faded, not until she departed from the chaos she'd created.

Lightning continued its violent streaks across the sky, painting spider webs among the dark clouds. Azure tilted her face to watch it, willing the gods to strike her down, but the sweet release of death never came for her. Instead, a large splash nearby sent the already tempestuous water washing over her. Startled, she moved further from the wreckage. She squinted into the darkness and watched as a man swam away from the remnants of the vessel and pulled himself onto one of the few rocks not covered in debris.

Adrenaline surged, her heart becoming lighter as she studied him. Even though it was forbidden, and a guaranteed death sentence, something told her to save him. Maybe if she saved this one life, it would make up for some of the atrocities she had committed over the last few years. It was a foolish wish in a life with no hope.

Heavy coughs racked the man's body as he held on for his life to the rock outcropping. Even as the massive waves assaulted him, he seemed determined to hold on. There was little doubt in Azure's mind that he was a fighter—a survivor. Something about him drew her in, making it impossible for her to look away. She couldn't bring herself to sacrifice him to the sea, even if rescuing him would lend to her own demise.

Her heart pounded erratically as she watched the man from the shadows, trying to convince herself to abandon him. If she saved him, she would be giving up on returning to her human life. She would be giving up on Daneliya. Realistically, she knew that the debt of five thousand souls was an unattainable goal anyway, because she could never harden her heart, nor steel herself enough, to continue wielding such death. Her sister would return to the ground and become dust before she would ever escape the Sea Goddess' clutches.

Reuniting with Daneliya had never felt so impossible, but saving this man? That was something she could do. An act of kindness that she hoped would ease the burden that weighed so heavily on her conscience. His ragged breathing grew heavier as his entire frame trembled. She wasn't sure if it was out of fear or exhaustion, but she knew that her window to act was growing smaller with each passing second.

Still, Azure continued to stare at him as she warred with indecision. His dark, drenched hair fell across his forehead, lending a fragile quality to his handsome face. His eyes fluttered open and closed as he fought the obvious exhaustion that threatened to pull him under.

The softness of his features, combined with his determination to survive, was enough for her mind to decide. Azure had little experience with men, having been pulled into the sea shortly after reaching adulthood, but this man called to her, even without his knowing, and she couldn't abandon him among the jagged rocks that had destroyed his ship and crew. Her life was *not* worth more than his, more than anyone's, but she couldn't save everyone. This man, though, she could save. Cutting through the water without another thought, Azure's strong tail propelled her through the powerful waves and toward a decision she couldn't take back.

As she darted toward the barely conscious man, she caught a glimpse of Oona in her peripheral vision. Moving stealthily toward them, Azure knew what the psychotic mermaid would do if she reached them. She would kill the man Azure intended to save and claim his soul for herself. Even if she had to give her own life, Azure would not allow that to happen, making a vow to herself at that moment. *He will not die tonight.* With no actual plan to keep that promise, she wrapped her arms around his semi-conscious form, gripping him tightly.

The moment his skin touched hers, a warmth radiated throughout her body, but she didn't have time to ponder the strange sensation, not until he was safe. She tried to pry him from the rocks, but he jerked away slightly, weak from his bid to live. His heavy-lidded eyes widened as he stared at her, incredulity and disbelief clear in his shocked expression.

"It's okay," she told him. "I'm going to get you out of here."

He remained unblinking as he nodded slowly, securing his arms around her neck before letting her pull him away from the tenuous safety of the rocks and into the dangers of the open sea.

Azure swam from the wreckage with his full weight on her shoulders. The man wasn't small, and he'd passed out shortly after grabbing onto her, but the added strength of her mermaid form, combined with the adrenaline coursing through her veins, made it easier to carry his weight as they cut through the water. His unconscious state, however, coupled with the frigid temperature of his body, frightened her. *What if she risked everything, and he died of hypothermia, anyway?*

Urgency to find a safe place for him fueled her. The violent seas made swimming a challenge, even though she could carry his weight. Usually, when the waters were so turbulent, she would have swum far below the surface and out of the current, but she couldn't do that with him in her arms. He would drown. So, setting her face in determination, and steadying her breaths against the pounding surf, Azure kept moving forward through the waves. It was the only way to save his life, as well as her own, which would be ripped from them if Oona or Lucia caught up.

The storm lessened in intensity after the crash, but it was still a worthy opponent. Aside from struggling against the weather, Azure couldn't help but worry about if Oona was following them. She just hoped the men in the water would serve as enough of a distraction for them to escape without pursuit. She had but one man, while the sea held dozens.

Taking him to the same cove she and Ocevia rested in was too risky, and she couldn't chance approaching the shore of the human cities, so she swam further out, hoping he could hold on for a bit longer. There were several islands dotting the sea that remained unoccupied because of their vast distances from the shipping channels. If she could make it to one of them, it would increase their odds of evading capture. If she got caught, she would be tortured and killed for stealing a soul from the Sea Goddess, as would he, so their only hope was to avoid detection. She never wanted to be a killer, and this was her chance to take a stand against her curse.

The dark shadows of the island loomed before them as they neared the shore, making the tension in Azure's body lessen, leaving behind exhaustion in its wake. She held the man's heavy form over her shoulder as she made the final movements of her tail, bringing them to the beach. He was still unconscious in her arms, but she whispered to him anyway, telling him he would be okay as she breathed in the intoxicating aroma of his masculine scent.

Azure struggled to slide his body onto the bank, the added pounding of the waves making it more of a challenge. Carrying him while swimming was one thing, but all her muscles were strained from the long journey, and she could barely support his weight above water. After finally managing to deposit him on the sand, she shifted into her human form and joined him on the shore.

Gazing down at the stranger, the sight of him lying there stilted her breath. Memories of Daneliya's lifeless body filled her mind's eye. Visions of her little sister's too blue lips and unmoving chest haunted her, and she retched violently, dropping to her knees as a sob escaped her. Once the dam broke, emotions flooded her, threatening to destroy her as she desperately tried to force them back. She warred with herself for a few moments before she locked the overwhelming pain away in her fractured, cursed heart.

Walking along the moonlit bank, Azure searched for kindling and dried logs, stifling shivers as a cool breeze blew across her wet skin. The islands were warm during the day, but without the coverings she stored in her usual cave, her damp body was completely nude and chilled to the bone, the shivers of her fear not helping to bring warmth. Once morning came, she would search the caves further inland in hopes of finding a breast band and bottoms long forgotten by another mermaid, but for now, fire was the priority. As cold as she was, Azure knew the human man would be near freezing without the magic of the curse to help him survive the lingering effects of the icy waters.

Watching the man tremble, still unconscious, she gathered the wood as fast as possible. She had not rescued him just for him to succumb to hypothermia. One of the first skills she had learned after becoming a mermaid was how to start a fire, so Azure had the flames licking against the driftwood she collected quickly. It wasn't a large fire, but it was enough to warm them, and hopefully too small to be spotted from afar.

She couldn't stop worrying about Oona and Lucia. If the vicious females found them, she and the man would be dragged to Miris without question. She hoped they had traveled far enough away for the duo to lose her trail. The sea was enormous, and the potential hideouts were endless. Unless they followed her, it was unlikely she would be found. At least that was her hope, which was all she had.

Once the fire was stable, Azure unstrapped his sword and dagger, setting them to the side before she removed his boots. She struggled as she tried to peel off his wet clothes, the drenched tunic and trousers clinging to his body, making it a slow process. The sea breeze and the insects would make him uncomfortable without clothes, so she was careful not to tear the fabrics as she stripped them off. She left his undergarments on to preserve his modesty but spread the rest of the soaked items across a large rock near the fire before returning to his side. Her eyes flicked over his chiseled body, mentally assuring herself that she was just checking to ensure his coloring looked normal. Her gaze merely lingered on his defined chest, and impressive stomach muscles, to make sure he still drew breath. The excuses were flimsy, even in her own mind, but she clung to them.

Having had very little experience with men, let alone semi-naked men, it was impossible for her not to admire him. Aside from the men who leaped into the sea to escape their sinking vessels, she'd never been so close to a man, and the unconscious one before her was more handsome than most.

She sat at his feet, rubbing from his calves down to his toes in a futile attempt to lend him some of her nonexistent warmth, as she took in his appearance. He was tall, his muscles firm and toned. His physique led her to believe he had plenty of practice with the sword she'd found strapped to him. Slow-drying rivulets of water slid down the hard planes of his stomach, drawing her gaze to the waistband of his undergarments, where they disappeared into the fabric. A large tattoo covered one of his pectorals, an image of a circular chain that was severed, the ends flaring out at the broken link.

She forced her eyes to return to his face, embarrassed at herself for openly admiring him without his knowledge, but her gaze didn't fall upon an unconscious man. When her eyes lifted to meet his face, he was staring back at her, curiosity clear in his expression.

Azure wondered what he was thinking. It couldn't be every day that he woke up drenched, in nothing but his underwear, on an uninhabited island with a naked stranger sitting at his feet. Her cheeks reddened as his stare dipped to her bare chest before darting back to her face once again. His eyes widened, and she knew it was because of her nakedness as much as because of his own semi-nudity and the unknown location.

"I was trying to warm you back up." She murmured as her hands stilled on his foot. "Your clothes were all wet. I didn't want you to die from hypothermia."

Turning his face toward the fire for a moment, he didn't pull his foot out of her hand. She started to massage his icy skin once more, hoping it would stimulate his blood flow as she waited for him to speak. The unending silence distressed her nerves.

After what felt like an eternity, she cleared her throat and drew his attention back from the dancing flames.

His gaze locked with hers, the deep blue of his eyes pulling her in as wholly as the call of the ocean. Her breath caught, and she had to steady herself before she spoke. "What's your name? I'm Azure."

He lifted himself onto his elbows, his movements stiff as he ran his fingers through his wet hair. "Elios... My name is Elios." He looked around again, but she knew there wasn't much he could see in the dim moonlight. "Where are we? How did I get here?"

"Oh." Mortified heat flooded Azure's cheeks, and she was glad for the darkness. How could she tell him that it was all her fault? "Your ship crashed, and I ... uh... saved you. I carried you here."

Head tilting to the side in confusion, Elios' stare turned incredulous. "How? I'm probably twice your weight, and the waves were intense. And where's the rest of the crew?"

Azure opened her mouth but closed it again without making a sound. Not knowing how to answer his questions without showing him her other form, she took a deep breath to steal her nerves. *It wasn't like she could hide that she was a mermaid from him forever, right?*

Her chest tightened like it was in a vise as she lowered her gaze to the ground at his feet. It was impossible to stare into his mesmerizing blue eyes and admit to murdering his crew. It was an unforgivable act, and, for some reason, she didn't want him to hate her. "The rest of your crew has probably already drowned." She knew they had drowned, felt their lights fizzle out when their souls entered the depths of the sea.

Azure clenched her fists to hide the tremors that wracked her hands, and stood, heading for the water. Sitting along the edge of the rising tide, the sea foam licked at her legs as she shifted them into a tail. Afraid of his reaction, she held her breath. She didn't speak as she waited for him to say something—*anything*—but he didn't. Elios just watched her, his intense stare raking over the length of her mermaid body. His blinking turned rapid, and she could see the moment when he realized what he was seeing was real, when he covered his mouth with his palm as he realized she wasn't human.

"This is how I managed to carry you to this island," she said. "As far as where we are... the best answer is a long way from the shipping channel and the shores of Thatia. Bringing you here was the best option." Hesitating, Azure gazed out at the sea blackened by night, hoping no eyes were watching her from the darkness. "I'm not allowed to approach the human lands. I brought you here because I thought you would be safe, but I admit it was a rushed decision. There wasn't much time to think. You needed to get out of the water before you froze to death."

Several agonizing moments of silence followed her rambling. She shifted back into her human form and returned to her seat near his feet again, unsure of what to say.

"What did my ship crash into? I thought the channel was clear." He still watched her, but his face softened. She exhaled slowly.

"There's a rock outcropping on the side of the channel. The ship veered off course and crashed into it. I saw you swimming away, trying to save yourself." She thought about mentioning her role in the wreck but decided against it. He wouldn't trust her if he knew she was responsible for murdering his companions and nearly killing him. There was a chance he would find out eventually, but she wasn't ready to divulge her guilt just yet. Their friendship, if it could even be called that, was too fragile. She couldn't get him to safety if he fought her every step of the way. Keeping the secret was the best course of action. *For now.*

Elios nodded, but his eyes were still full of questions. Questions she could, but wouldn't, answer.

"So, what now?"

That was the one inquiry she didn't have a response to. There was no time for her to concoct a solid plan before, or after, she'd saved him from the rocks. Traveling undetected by her enemies, and saving his life, had dominated her thoughts as they fled.

"My only plan for now is to keep you alive. That's been my plan since I pulled you from the rocks."

"Well, aside from having no way back to shore, I guess I'm okay. Alive. So, thank you."

A cool breeze blew over the island just as she contemplated his statement. He rubbed his arms for warmth against the wind, and she rose to add more wood to the fire, deciding to share the truth about herself, at least some of it. "I guess there is something you need to know about mermaids."

His eyebrows furrowed. "Okay."

She swallowed back her hesitation. "We're all slaves to the Sea Goddess, Miris. We were taken from our human lives to fulfill a debt, after striking a bargain with her."

His features fell, but his eyes were kind. Fixated on tending to the fire, she tried to avoid the pity in his gaze. She wasn't asking for his sympathy. She didn't deserve it. "Why were you taken? What was your debt for?"

Azure poked at the burning logs with a stick, watching the flurry of embers she knocked loose as they cascaded through the darkness. She wasn't comfortable being vulnerable and admitting her truth to him made her feel far more exposed than her nude state ever could.

Taking a deep breath, she exhaled slowly. "Three years ago, my little sister..." Squeezing her eyes shut, she inhaled again, trying to steady her shaking voice. Speaking of that day always brought the painful memory to the surface so intensely that she felt like she was reliving the nightmare. "My little sister, Daneliya, drowned. We were on the beach, and I looked away. It was only for a second, just a second, but..." She trailed off, suppressing the tears burning behind her eyes. Shame coursed through her as images of the lifeless child flashed across the back of her closed lids. It was all her fault. Daneliya's death, although temporary, and her own cursed enslavement. It was all because of her. "She was only seven years old."

Elios moved closer and placed a callused hand on hers. Tears rolled down her cheeks as she opened her eyes and looked up at him. "I'm so sorry you lost your sister. That's such a tragedy. I can't imagine what that was like for you."

She sniffled and vigorously wiped at her damp cheeks. "She didn't remain dead." His hand seemed to stiffen against hers, but he remained silent. "Miris appeared on the beach as I cried over Daneliya's lifeless body... as I screamed for help. She offered to save my sister if I traded my life for hers. I didn't know what that meant, but I agreed, anyway." It was becoming increasingly difficult to keep her voice stable as flashbacks of that day assaulted her mind. "I couldn't let her die. Miris brought my sister back to life, but I was turned into a monster in exchange. I could either accept my life like this or die and never have even the slightest chance of seeing Daneliya again."

He squeezed her hand gently, the gesture unexpected. "You're not a monster, Azure." His tone was so understanding and genuine that she cringed. If he only knew the things she'd done, he would hate her. Her chest tightened as more tears fell.

"I wasn't, not until I made the deal with Miris. Our curse... mermaids are forced to repay our debts with souls. We have to kill if we ever hope to be free. If I'd known before..." Lingering on the thought, she shook her head in disgust at herself. "If I had known that I would have to claim five thousand lives to retrieve my own, I would've died that first night. I would've never stepped foot in the sea. Living like this? Being a monster? It isn't worth it."

Elios pulled his hand away from hers and rubbed his forehead. The absence of his touch hurt, another wound on her battered heart.

"You have to kill five thousand people?" His question cut her like a knife, although his tone was more questioning than accusatory. The burning taste of dread coated her throat again, but she nodded.

"Most mermaids don't kill with their own hands. We create situations that result in casualties instead."

Afraid to see the disgust she felt for herself mirrored in his expression, Azure stood and walked to the shoreline. She stared out at the dark waters, watching the gentle tide rolling in. The chaos of the storm had faded, but the calm sea made her anxious. If they were followed, it would've been easy to find them now. She desperately hoped she'd lost Oona, but until they moved further from the shipping channel, she wouldn't be able to relax. The murderous mermaid could have been watching them at that moment, and Azure wouldn't know unless she showed herself. By then, it would have been too late.

"What happened to your back?" Without her realizing, Elios had closed the distance between them. She looked over her shoulder and flinched as she saw how intently he focused on her marred flesh. Turning to face him, she wished he hadn't seen her wounds. It was too hard to stomach his pity when his current situation was her fault.

"That's what happens when you disobey Miris. Just because I'm cursed doesn't mean I want to kill. Disobedience doesn't go unpunished."

Reaching for her, he took her hand again, sending a surge of awareness through her body, and when their stares locked, she knew he felt it too. The blue of his eyes seemed to deepen at the simple touch. "Will you be whipped for saving me?"

Azure licked her lips, desperate for moisture, but her mouth was completely dry. She cleared her throat before she answered, resolving to tell him the whole truth this time. "Saving a sacrifice has never happened, not to my knowledge, but Miris is cruel. She'll torture me, and then either add to my debt or kill me. Probably the former. I'm worth too much to her to kill." She smirked; the irony not lost on her. How long has she prayed for death? "Killing me would give me what I want, so I doubt she'd give me that mercy, but she could surprise me."

His gaze hardened with a determination she couldn't understand. "And what about me?"

That was the part that worried her most. His soul was more valuable than her cursed existence. His determination, his sheer resolve to survive, was the reason she'd saved him in the first place. With every mark carved on that cave wall, her life became more worthless, but this man wanted to live—*deserved to live*. "That's why I chose an island so far from the wreckage. You were supposed to die tonight. Miris is greedy. To her, your soul is already hers to claim. She'll have her henchmen hunting for you. We need to move farther away soon, but honestly, I'm not sure where we can go to escape them. Mermaids aren't allowed to go into the human lands, but Miris would let her people do so if it meant retrieving the sacrifice that was stolen from her. I'm not sure where you, or I, would be safe."

Elios rubbed his face again, worry coating his features. "So, our only option is to run? To keep running?"

Nodding, she turned her attention to the water, scanning for unseen threats. "Until I figure something else out, yes."

Azure took a deep breath before turning away from the midnight-colored sea and back to his handsome face. Squeezing his clammy hand in hers, she tugged gently. After so much time in the water, he was still too exposed. "Come back to the fire. You're freezing." Leading Elios back to the steady flames, she sat beside him.

"So, when do we leave?" His grip tightened minutely, as though the touch reassured him as much as it reassured her. She shrugged a single shoulder as she stared at the driftwood turning into ash.

"We'll hide in the cave once the sun rises and we can look for food and something I can use as clothes. My people tend to store items in caverns for when they stop to rest, so I'm hoping there is a stash here somewhere. I've never traveled beyond this point, so I don't know what other islands or caves exist farther out. Hopefully, we can find somewhere safe to hide out for a few days. For now, you should try to get some rest."

"You should as well."

"I would feel better keeping watch."

Elios smiled, cocking his head to the side. It was the first time she'd seen such an easy-going expression on his face, and it made him so attractive her heart skipped a beat. "I would feel better knowing you won't pass out from exhaustion while we travel tomorrow. I can't exactly swim to another island by myself."

Her eyebrows shot up. His dire words were at odds with his playful tone. She scanned the island, wanting to put his mind at ease. Maybe, if they put out the fire, and moved further away from shore, they would be hidden enough to be safe. Still, Azure didn't like the idea. It was far too risky for Elios to brave the elements without a fire. They didn't know how large the island was, or what types of creatures lived on it. "It would be too uncomfortable for you, between the breeze and the bugs. We would have to put out this fire and venture into the caves to be able to let both of our guards down. Plus, there could be predators within the caves. My kind is not the only threat. I'll just stay awake tonight."

He glanced at the inland caves and squared his shoulders, seeming to take her words as a challenge, rather than a warning. "We can share body heat if we must. And you're not the only one who can protect us." He reached for his weapons. "If we have to fight, I can help."

Azure tucked a lock of violet-tinged black hair behind her ear, biting her lower lip as she considered his words. She would rather keep watch, but he was right. Exhaustion already made her limbs feel heavy, and she would need rest in order to travel the next day. Carrying his extra weight was one thing, but if they had to shake off any pursuers, it would be best if she was energized. "Alright. If you're sure."

"I am."

"Okay. Let's grab your things and put the fire out. Then we can try to find a place to sleep." Standing before Azure finished speaking, Elios reached down and helped her to her feet. He fashioned a makeshift torch before kicking sand into the fire. It sent up a flurry of embers and then died out, nothing but smoke remaining.

She collected his still damp clothing while he grabbed his boots and weapons. He smiled at her again, and her heart fluttered once more. They worked as a team, and it gave her hope they might somehow survive this predicament. She hadn't realized she was staring until he said, "are we ready?"

"Oh, yeah. Sorry." Shaking her head to clear it, Azure reached for his hand, leading the way across the poorly lit beach.

Chapter Four
Finding Shelter

T he trek across the wild island was far easier with Elios' makeshift torch. Azure spotted three caves in the distance; her cursed eyes stronger than his human ones. Though the caverns varied in size, there was no sign that any of them were occupied. Although they couldn't be sure what was hidden within them. The cave on the right and one in the center shared an entrance that fissured off into two smaller sections. Choosing the joint entrance first, but peeking inside the secondary opening closest to them, Azure realized it wasn't a safe option. The depth was not enough to hide them adequately.

She heaved a disappointed sigh and waited as Elios gathered the few supplies that had been left behind by one of her people. Once he finished, Azure pulled him toward the other cave inside the split entrance. She hoped it was larger, something that could serve as multiple rooms and hide them from prying eyes.

The second cave was indeed bigger than the first, but it was a wide-open cavern that would leave them with no way to hide themselves if any other mermaids stumbled upon the island. If they could find no other options, it would have to serve as shelter from the weather and a place to light a fire, but it left them vulnerable to intruders. It wasn't a place they could defend.

They left the dual entrance without a solid plan for refuge, but at least they had a few pieces of clothing, some dried fish, and a makeshift blanket. Azure dressed in the spare fabric before the pair moved into the next cave, hoping they would find a suitable hideout there. It was impossible to survey the inside of the third cave because of a large boulder blocking the entrance, but there was an opening big enough for a person to crawl through. The blocked off cavern would have offered additional security if they could manage to climb inside, provided the interior chamber was sizable enough for them to rest comfortably.

Pondering what awaited them beyond the boulder could only get them so far. Azure straightened her spine and handed the torch to Elios before wriggling through the gap. It was dark inside, making it impossible to get a good look, so she stuck her hand back out through the crack she'd crawled through, and asked for the solitary flame that served as their only light source.

Elios handed it over, and she held it high to let the soft beams illuminate as much of the space as possible. The hidden entrance made Azure wonder if they could remain on the island longer. It would give them time to rest and regroup before they ventured further out to sea. Once they left the island, there was no way of knowing how far they would have to travel before finding another sanctuary.

She shook off her revolving thoughts and rearranged some of the stones that blocked the opening, hoping to widen the narrow gap enough for Elios to crawl through. It was still a tight squeeze, his body much larger than hers, but after a moment of determination, and some awkward contorting on his part, the large man joined her within the chamber.

The primary room was larger than she'd expected. It had a tall cathedral ceiling with a small opening that would provide ventilation, the perfect room for lighting fires if they chose their kindling carefully to minimize the smoke.

Gingerly, Azure made her way around the perimeter, with Elios trailing behind her, his hand resting on her bare shoulder as a guide. The torch cast sinister shadows against the rock faces, as she silently hoped there were no animals calling this space home. To her relief, aside from desiccated droppings and aged animal bones, the cave was empty.

As they ventured further, the shadows contorted against the back wall of the cave. Azure's eyes caught on the strange bend silhouetted in the corner, and she stared, trying to determine what was so off about it. As they moved closer, she realized there was a gap in what had, at first glance, appeared to be the back of the cave. Her heartbeat quickened as she examined the unexpected feature.

"It looks like an opening to another chamber," Elios murmured, moving closer to where the wall broke into a small bend. His chest hovered a fraction of an inch from her, and she found herself wishing he'd move closer. Silly really, considering the lashing that still scarred her flesh, but still, the warmth he radiated made her belly clench. He peered over her shoulder as she dipped the torch into the corridor beyond. "I don't know where this leads, but it could be a good home for animals. Or for us."

Setting down their supplies, Elios drew his dagger before taking the torch from her. "I'll check it out. Stay here until I give the all-clear."

She didn't like the idea of him searching the unknown space alone, but she let him go first, since he was the only one with a weapon. After he disappeared into the gap, Azure scooped up the supplies he'd left behind and followed him into the darkened corridor.

Their footsteps were near silent as they crept forward, the sound of their breaths the only thing to reach her ears. Without warning, Elios halted in front of her, causing her to collide with his muscled back. In the faint flicker of the torch's light, she saw him place a finger to his lips, and she stiffened at the nonverbal command. She hadn't sensed any threat, but she held her breath and trusted his instincts.

After a few seconds, she heard faint rhythmic taps upon stone.

"Do you hear that?" Elios whispered. He was so close his lips brushed against the shell of her ear as his warm breath skittered across her face. She nodded, too tense to respond. "I think it's dripping water."

Azure's fear turned into excitement at the statement, and they resumed their jaunt into the darkness.

After a few more minutes, the corridor opened into a secondary chamber and Elios was right about the water. The dripping sound grew louder, echoing throughout the enclosed space. At first glance, they couldn't determine where it was coming from. No moonlight streamed into the isolation of the rear chamber, and the abyss that surrounded them was no more than a black void. The torch had grown weaker the longer it burned, barely illuminating a foot in front of them.

They circled the room at a painfully slow pace, hoping the small steps would prevent them from rushing upon an animal or slipping on the damp ground. The monotony of the stone wall broke as it curved back, and the floor dipped to reveal a pool of water being fed by several streams that trailed down the wall from the ceiling.

"This place is amazing," Elios said as he stooped down to submerge his hand. "It's warm. Do you think this is a hot spring?"

"It's possible. Although we're in the middle of the sea, there are plenty of volcanoes nearby that could cause this. They likely caused all the islands."

Elios straightened his legs and headed for the other side of the chamber. "It should be safe to start a fire here. There's plenty of space, and the ceiling is high."

"I was wondering the same thing. My only concern is ventilation, but we can try a small one first." Azure shifted her weight as she scanned the room, her eyes adjusting to the darkness as time passed. "This cave is way more secure than I thought it would be. Even if someone looked for us, odds are they'd only search the caves that aren't blocked. If they come into this one, they wouldn't see the entrance to this back chamber if we closed it properly. It may be safe to stay here longer if we don't spot any activity nearby."

A slow smile spread across Elios' face. "With all the trees that surround the caves, there must be resources. Well, if the water dripping down the wall is drinkable. If not, we might need to find a way to collect rainwater."

Elios' positivity was refreshing. He rolled with the punches instead of dwelling on his misfortunes, and it made warmth spread through Azure's chest. She wished she could be so positive.

"Should we gather wood, then?"

Elios' grin widened as he took her hand. "Let's do it."

Leading their way back through the labyrinth, Elios was the first to step back out into the night air. Azure wasn't sure of the time, but the sun still slumbered, and the waning torch barely lit their path. The moon illuminated their journey to the forest but was blocked by the dense canopy as soon as they entered the tree line.

The island was larger than Azure had expected, most of it heavily treed. Kindling was plentiful, so they collected as many sticks and twigs as they could carry before retreating to the safety of the cave.

Elios began building the fire as soon as they returned to the rear chamber. Azure hadn't even had a chance to set her wood down before he had sparked the first flame within their makeshift fire pit. He continued to surprise her, and she wondered where he'd learned such impressive survival skills. It seemed at odds with the fact that he was a merchant sailor. Perhaps he wasn't on that ship for work. Some men purchased passage on merchant vessels in order to visit far-away lands. That seemed far more cohesive to his personality, but she didn't have the nerve to pry.

She knew little about him, though he made her quite curious. Surely, she would get to know him while they hid away together. The thought made her smile.

After the fire was crackling, warming, and illuminating the stone chamber, Elios checked the water that trailed from the wall into the pool below, determining it wasn't saltwater from the sea. Azure could not believe their luck. Somehow, out of all the islands scattered throughout the Lamalis Sea, they had escaped to one with a hot spring. It was a tremendous benefit, and an excellent reason to remain on the island for as long as they could. As long as it was safe.

Sitting beside the fire for warmth, the pair shared some of the dried fish they'd found while searching the other caverns. Azure hated the staple food of her people, but she forced it down, anyway. They were lucky to have food at all. After they ate, they washed up in the warm water, and Elios put his barely dried trousers back on. Azure was used to the chill of the sea, but humans were not built to withstand it. So, although Elios insisted that she take the blanket, she pushed the fabric back at him. He chuckled as he suggested they share, an offer she was hesitant to accept.

They spent the night tucked between the back wall and the fire, lying next to each other, but not making any physical contact. She wanted to touch him desperately, but she didn't understand why the desire was so strong. She knew little about him, but something about him called to her. Maybe it was her own deep-down desire for love and companionship. They would have to go their separate ways once she ensured he was safe, so there was no use dwelling on it. She was cursed to remain in the sea, and he was human. Any hope for love was no more than a fantasy.

Azure had never wanted a man before. A lover never interested her, but Elios was different. His scent, alone, was enough to make her want to nuzzle into his neck and never come up for air. But she didn't let her cravings get the better of her. Instead, she laid on top of the blanket while he burrowed beneath it and tended to the fire while he slept. She was tired, but he'd nearly drowned. He needed the rest far more than she did. Since they intended to stay on the island longer, she decided she would nap during the daylight hours to make up for her lack of sleep. Her needs were not more urgent than his were.

Even with the resources and safety features of their current hideout, the desire to flee the island, and keep running, still burned inside of her. Her survival instincts still pulled her in another direction, begging her to keep putting distance between them and the crash site.

Worries plagued her as she watched the flames lick at the darkness. Her mind whirled with potential outcomes, both on their current island and off it. Weapons were taking priority in her mind. If they had more ways to defend themselves, maybe she would feel more at ease. Elios possessed a sword and a dagger, but she had nothing. Miris would send out scouts to locate them first. One or two mermaids would hunt them down before the goddess unleashed her forces to capture them. If they could spot and dispose of the scouts, maybe it would prolong their lives, increase their chances of survival.

T hey were too far back in the cave's depth to see the sun rise, but Elios' bright blue eyes flitting open was enough to signal the start of their day. Azure already itched to leave the confined space, so his eyes opening could not have come soon enough. He grinned at her as he rubbed the sleep away. His rich brown hair was ruffled from his slumber, giving him a boyish look that melted her icy heart.

"Good morning," he said as he sat up. "How did you sleep?"

Azure glanced toward the fire that still burned with the fresh wood she'd added only a short time before he woke. "Not much, honestly. I kept the fire going and had a lot on my mind."

His smile fell, making her regret her words. She didn't need to add to his worries. "You need your rest, too. I'll do fire duty tonight."

She waved him off. "It's okay, really. I'm used to working at night and resting during the day." She paused, knowing her *work* killed his friends. "I can take a nap later."

Elios nodded as he reached for his boots. "That's a good idea. What were you thinking about?"

Azure turned to him, pursing her lips. "What do you mean?"

"You said you had a lot on your mind last night. I was just curious what you were thinking about?"

Clearing her throat, the fire suddenly became the most interesting thing in the room. She stared at the dancing flames, avoiding his inquisitive gaze. "If we're going to stay here longer, we need to make more weapons. Mermaids sleep for most of the day since our nights are so long. Well, unless Miris is making them search for us. We should spend the late afternoons and nights hidden away, just in case. If the Sea Goddess has already sent scouts out to look for us, we need to be prepared. I'm not sure how long we can stay here. We're still pretty close to her underwater caves and the main shipping channels."

She could tell Elios was considering what she said by how his eyebrows scrunched together. He scratched his chin absently.

As he remained quiet for a few moments, Azure stared at the stubble that shadowed his chin and cheeks. Anxiously awaiting his response, she returned her gaze to the fire.

"We could probably sharpen rocks to use as blades and fit them with wood to make knives or spears. Here," he said as he offered his dagger to her. "You can use this for now."

Azure reached for the sheathed blade and tucked it against her chest. It was too dark in the cave to examine the knife, even with the fire burning, but her tension eased marginally just by having it in her hand. She didn't have much experience wielding weapons but being armed made her feel better.

"Thank you."

Elios nodded and smiled at her as he finished lacing his boot. She continued speaking as she stood. "Should we go outside and get our day started? I would feel better if we collected supplies quickly and returned to the cave right away. Especially today. They will almost certainly be searching for us today."

Climbing to his feet, Elios grabbed her hand before lighting a torch. She leaned heavily into him. The lack of sleep was weighing her down more than she'd realized, and she swayed as they headed for the exit. In her current state, she would have been useless in a fight, and she knew it. Sleep needed to be more of a priority before night fell, so she could keep watch over Elios as he slept again.

His hand remained firmly around hers as he led their way outside. She knew she had better night vision than a human, but she kept that to herself. She enjoyed his touch too much.

Elios tapped out the makeshift torch as soon as they stepped into the daylight, preserving it for later. The sun was still making her way up into the sky, but it was already a bright day. The storms of the night before were long gone and a soft breeze rolled in off the sea, keeping the morning heat from becoming too stifling. Elios was fully dressed in his now dry clothes, but Azure wore merely a breast wrap and a loincloth. Her lack of coverage, in comparison, made her self-conscious, but as they stumbled along the rocky terrain and into the forested area, she regretted not having shoes the most.

Chapter Five
The Island

T he forest was lush and radiant. Its canopy comprised a collection of oak, palm, and fruit trees that Azure had never seen before. Beams of sunlight filtered through, scattering across the forest floor and giving life to the colorful mushrooms that ruled the stony grounds below. Swirling vines encircled most of the trees, and a mishmash of flowers desperately tried to avoid the shadows, highlighting the otherwise jade landscape. Chirping birds filled the air with their cheery melody, brightening the atmosphere of the forest, but were drowned out by the occasional wave as they crashed upon the shore.

Closing her eyes, Azure took in the forest's natural scent. It had been so long since she'd explored a land so much like the one she had lived in before her world came crashing down, before she was yanked from her life with her sister. A familiar ache of longing developed in her heart, making her chest heavy.

"Here." Azure opened her eyes and saw Elios smiling down at her, holding a large egg-shaped piece of green and orange fruit. "Are you hungry?"

Giggling, she hugged him on impulse before grabbing the fruit. She stepped back, cheeks flushed, when she realized what she'd just done. "You found a mango! Thank you! They're my favorite!"

His broad grin showed no signs that he'd minded the sudden show of affection, even though they barely knew each other. Her blush deepened as she brought the mango to her lips and bit into its firm skin, pulling to strip the section off. The sweet juice exploded in her mouth, dripping down her chin, continuing its trail to the top of her chest, but she didn't care. After a never-ending diet of fish, she would happily bathe in tangy nectar as long as some of it landed in her mouth. He chuckled and reached out his hand.

"Hand me the dagger, and I'll cut that for you." She realized, in that moment, that she'd been so lost in the dulcet flavor of the mango that she probably looked ridiculous. Dragging her forearm across her face to clear the remnants, she only made it worse, leaving a smear of stickiness in its wake.

Handing the dagger to Elios, Azure watched as he peeled away the thick skin of the fruit. She was excited to dig into the juicy mango, but she tried to wait patiently as he sliced off a sizable chunk and handed it to her. Her eyes practically rolled back in her head as soon as it touched her tongue.

Sharing two more mangoes, they set off in search of supplies. Making weapons was the priority, but they kept their eyes peeled for anything that could prove useful. After they'd finished scavenging in the forest, they scanned the beach.

With waves constantly hitting the shore, there were lots of items that found their way onto the sand. They completed their eclectic collection with several glass bottles that could be used for drinking, a large piece of leather, and a torn sail that could be repurposed. Piling their treasures, stones, and extra wood outside the cave entrance, they headed back to the forest one more time. After the pair collected as much fruit as they could reasonably carry, Elios wrapped everything in the damaged sail, and they returned to the relative safety of the cave.

It took several trips through the small opening to bring their entire bounty inside, but it was safer to remain hidden as much as they could. They collected enough food and firewood to last them for a few days. Miris would continue to search for them, but Azure hoped the scouts would move beyond their location by the time she and Elios needed to venture out again. If they stayed within the relative safety of their temporary home, the mermaids sent to find them would likely believe the island was uninhabited and continue their search elsewhere. At least, that was Azure's hope.

Once the last of their goods were deposited beside the hot spring, they got to work. Elios used his dagger to carve a long branch into a spear handle while Azure stripped part of the leather. Their teamwork made Azure's stomach flutter. They were hardly more than strangers, yet they worked together as though they had known each other for years.

When she'd rescued Elios, she didn't know what kind of man he was, but she was relieved to know he was at least handy. She held no doubt when it came to his abilities. Surely, she had saved the best man on the ship, as awful as that sounded.

"What are you thinking about?" Elios' voice pulled her from her thoughts. She glanced up to find him watching her.

"Not much. Just trying to turn this section of leather into proper clothing. Something with a bit more coverage than what we found in the cave."

His eyes dropped to her chest for a fraction of a second before he seemed to catch himself and lifted his eyes to meet hers again, a mischievous grin playing at his lips. The reaction wasn't one she expected, and she blushed, assuming he liked what she was wearing just fine. Still, if she had to fight, she would have preferred to do it without her breasts popping out.

"Do you need some help?"

Her heart thundered at his offer, although his face was genuine. She shook her head. "Since I have no thread, it won't take long. I'm just going to cut this and close it with knots. How are the weapons coming along?"

A regretful look on his face, Elios flourished the roughly made spear in front of him. The branch's surface had been smoothed, but he was just beginning to sharpen a stone for the tip.

"It's getting there. The branches are sturdy, so that's a plus, but it'll take some time to sharpen the stones without the proper tools."

Azure studied his desolate expression before turning her back on him. She untied the skimpy breast band she wore and replaced it with the leather cover she'd made, tying the two ends into a knot below her breasts. The top was nothing more than a leather wrap with haphazardly cut arm holes that covered her chest but offered some support. She was glad that her breasts were not large, or the cover would have been useless. The bottom piece she created was nothing more than a slightly larger loincloth that she knotted in place at her hip and covered with another strip as a skirt. When she turned around, he was looking at her from the corner of his eye while knocking two stones together.

"Okay. Now I can help you with the weapons."

Seeming to be lost in his thoughts when she spoke, Elios shook his head from side to side as if to clear it.

"That, um, that would be great." The fire was the only source of light in the cave, but she still saw the rosiness blooming across his cheeks, and it heated her own. Trying to ignore how self-conscious she felt, Azure sat next to him and held out her hand.

"Tell me how to help." He stared at her hand for a moment before placing a long piece of wood and a rough stone into it.

"Sand this down, and we can use it to make another spear."

Nodding, she turned her attention to the task, but felt his gaze linger on her for another moment before he returned to his own work.

The cave grew increasingly hot as time wore on. Between the warm spring day outside and the fire crackling near them, it was almost stifling. Still, they kept the flame steady for the light. Elios removed his tunic, and it became harder for Azure to concentrate. She found herself watching as beads of sweat glistened and slid down his chiseled chest. Ignoring the view was impossible, but she tried her best to focus on her work.

They took a brief lunch break, nibbled on a bit of fruit, and decided to create smaller fires around the chamber to allow for more light without the sweltering heat of a solitary fire. Azure felt instant relief once they banked the main blaze. The smaller fires had to be tended to more regularly, but they provided a welcomed escape from the thick darkness and sweltering heat.

The pair chatted as they worked, discussing the best ways to create weapons with what they had and making mental lists of what they would need to look for when they scavenged again. Azure yearned to know more about him, about his family. She wanted to know why he was on that merchant vessel, and where he was from, but she couldn't find the courage to ask.

Her skin prickled with unease as the hours wore on, knowing Miris' people were searching for them, but she tried not to let it show. She didn't want to worry him more, so she put on a brave face, far braver than she felt. Sitting in the dark, quiet space gave her thoughts room to whirl, zapping her of her meager energy stores. She hadn't had time to sleep yet, and it was taking its toll.

"Do you know how to use a spear? Any weapons?"

Azure jolted awake at the sound of Elios' voice. She had not realized she'd drifted off until then. It seemed neither had he. She shook her head, more to wake herself than to answer his question. Although, the answer was still no.

"I was cursed at eighteen." Thinking about Daneliya and her old life was a knife in her gut, but she pushed her sister's face into the depths of her consciousness, trying to lessen the blow. "Up until then, I'd never needed a weapon. Once I became this." She motioned toward herself, disgust creeping into her tone. "I definitely didn't need them."

Elios watched her face in silence, his own falling. Standing, he handed her one of the new spears and gave her a sympathetic smile. She appreciated his attempt to change the subject, but she struggled to let go of the overwhelming self-loathing that plagued her heart. *It always plagued her heart.*

Azure eyed the weapon warily before standing and taking it. The spear was heavier than she'd expected, but surprisingly well-balanced, especially with how roughly it was made.

"How do you catch fish if not with a spear? Do you use nets?"

She shrugged a shoulder as she switched the handle from hand to hand, avoiding his intense stare. "I found a net that washed up on shore. It's stored in the cave I use most of the time. It works well enough, but I can catch them with my hands... if I have to."

Elios smirked, his eyebrows raised, and grabbed a spear of his own. "When it's safe to go out again, I need to see that. I don't think I've ever seen someone catch a live fish with their bare hands."

For the first time in three years, Azure was excited to get back into the water, if only to impress him. She was quite skilled at catching the slippery creatures.

Elios gave her a moment's notice before swinging his spear at her, forcing her to forget about showing off and block the blow. The scattered fires made maneuvering within the space difficult, but their dangerous dance around the cave brought some life back into her sleepy limbs.

Once their impromptu sparring came to an end, Elios showed her the basics. From how to hold the spear, to how to block an attack, even showing her how to wield his sword and throw a dagger. He tailored her lessons to the meager skills she'd shown, and it was amazing how much she learned. He consistently reminded her that when all else failed, she needed to just jab the pointy end into her enemy. His instructions were as appreciated as they were fun. Practicing helped her to gain some confidence, a drop of it in an empty bucket. She couldn't defeat an enemy yet but working her muscles to where sweat glistened against her skin released at least some of the anxieties of their situation.

Once the moon rose high in the sky, Azure and Elios journeyed outside again, this time to grab more wood and stones so they could obscure the small opening of the cave's hidden entrance. They hadn't planned to venture out again so soon, but they'd discussed covering the cave's entrance during their sparring and realized it was a necessity if they were to remain safe. In theory, the branches would make noise if anyone tried to enter, allowing them a warning if their sanctuary was breached.

The idea of having an alarm system in place made her feel better about sleeping at the same time as Elios. The large boulders at the entrance were too heavy for one person to move, and the added wood and stones would make it appear as though no one was inside the cave because of an impassable entry point. They would have to move it all out of the way whenever they left the cave, but it was worth the trouble for the added security.

When they returned to the cave, they cut a large piece of sail and used a few branches to fasten a crude privacy screen in the back corner of the cave for when they needed to relieve themselves. Foliage was gathered for bedding, something to place under the leather to soften their makeshift bed. If they were able to stay for a while, they wanted the space to be as cozy as possible.

By the time they'd built a larger fire, leaving the smaller ones burning for light, Azure's limbs were sore. Trying to ignore how filthy she was, she'd sat next to Elios while they shared dried fish and fruit for their supper. Her hygiene wasn't ideal, but it didn't bother her much. They were in a relatively safe space, and she was in good company. It was more than she dared hope for when she pulled a drowning man from the unforgiving sea.

"Do you want to bathe first or should I?" Elios asked, rinsing the fruit's nectar from his dagger. Azure shrugged.

"You've already seen me naked." Her face heated as she remembered the way his drenched undergarments clung to his body. She might have only seen him *mostly* naked, but little had been left to the imagination. "So, it doesn't matter. I don't care if we clean up at the same time. The pool is big enough. Whatever you're most comfortable with."

The attraction was undeniable, even if they'd only just met. Her lack of experience meant nothing when it came to the way he made her feel. When she'd pulled him from the water, a bond was created between them, one that would last a lifetime. She wondered if he felt it, too. It felt like she was meant to see him that night—to save him.

When Azure looked up, she caught Elios' gaze, catching him scanning her face. He didn't speak, but he looked like he was trying to decide if she was being serious or not. *She was.*

Neither entered the pool right away. Maybe she was being reckless in suggesting they bathe together, but she wasn't promised to see another day. If these were some of her last moments, she didn't want any regrets. She wouldn't deny herself more than she'd already been denied in her life.

"What?" she asked, moving toward the water while loosening the knot on her top.

The last three years had been a blur of misery, and there was nothing for her to look forward to but more of the same. In all likelihood, Miris would eventually find them, and she would die. With the guillotine looming over her, she decided to open herself up to the pleasures of life while with Elios. She didn't know if he had a woman back home, but there was no ring on his finger, and he'd never mentioned a wife, even when he had almost died. That gave her some comfort, at least.

One more knot was untied, and Azure's loincloth fell to her feet. She left it there, not looking back at Elios as she stepped into the warm water. The natural pool was not overly large, but it was big enough.

When she chanced a glance at Elios, he was still standing in the same spot, but his boots were off. He peered at her, undeniable curiosity on his face. With lips slightly parted, he shifted his weight before moving closer.

"Are you sure you don't mind? I, uh..." He ran his fingers through his dark hair and retreated a step. "I don't mind going back to the fire and waiting."

Azure enjoyed his nervousness. Being inexperienced, it felt good to have the upper hand in their flirtation. Her movements were slow and exaggerated. She enjoyed the feel of his eyes drinking in her naked body as she wet her hair, her breasts jutting out of the water when she leaned back.

His stumbling fueled her bravery, surprising her at her own actions. She rubbed her breasts under the guise of cleaning them, but the subtle touch sent a bolt of electricity straight to her groin as she held his cerulean stare. The fact that she hardly knew him continued to rear its ugly head in her mind, but she pushed it away every single time. These weren't normal circumstances.

With death seeking them, there was absolutely nothing to lose. She threw caution, and modesty, to the wind as she ran her hands over her wet hair. Elios hovered beside the pool, open-mouthed and unblinking, like he was waiting for a sign that she truly wanted him to join her, as though her words hadn't already been indication enough. She chuckled to herself before standing. The water sloshed down her body as she rose on the tips of her toes, exposing as much of her nude flesh as possible before shifting her legs into an iridescent purple tail.

"I meant what I said, Elios. I don't mind."

Although her shifting seemed to catch him by surprise, her reassurance was enough for him. Untying the waistband of his trousers, he pulled them down and kicked them to the floor. The small fires around the chamber were hardly more than embers now, but the dull light was enough to take him in. She devoured him with her gaze, licking her lips in a desperate bid to return the moisture that dried up at the sight. He was more handsome each time she looked at him. And below his waist, she didn't even dare to glance.

Elios lowered himself into the water, dunking under the surface. They didn't have soap, but they did have Juniper berries, which were used in soap-making. Azure grabbed a handful of the berries from the ledge beside her and brought them over to where Elios was still submerged, her tail luxuriating in the warm water. She set them on the side of the pool and moved to return to her spot, but before she could pass where he bubbled below the surface, he reemerged in front of her.

Their eyes locked, and her heart hammered as she waited for him to break the stare. She was too afraid to kiss him, didn't even know how, but far too tempted in the moment to simply walk away. The side of his mouth lifted into a half-smile as he leaned forward. Her lips parted in anticipation of his lips on hers, but he only reached past her to grab the berries, smashing them in his hand.

Her shoulders slumped in disappointment as she swam back to the other side of the pool. There was no way he had not realized she wanted him to kiss her, or maybe he really hadn't. It wasn't like they knew each other. Maybe he thought it was bad timing. It was bad timing, after all. They were hiding in a cave, on the run with their lives on the line, no more than strangers. It wasn't just bad timing. It was the *worst* timing.

But still, she wanted him, regardless of their circumstances. Maybe he really did have a woman at home, or maybe she misinterpreted the way he looked at her. Maybe she was the only one who felt the connection between them when they touched.

Returning to her place in the pool, Azure rubbed the berries into her hair, her back to Elios. She was lost in thought as she scrubbed, hating herself for acting like a lovesick child. Nothing in her life prepared her for a romantic relationship, and it wasn't as if she deserved one, anyway. Still, a pit opened in her chest, and she didn't know how to fill it. Her tail shifted back to legs as she washed, her legs needing the bath as much as her tail needed the water. When she turned around, full of self-loathing and insecurity, Elios was only a foot away from her. He was so close that she could feel his breath. Her pulse quickened.

"Are you angry with me?" The look he gave her was one of concern. She felt the authenticity of his worry in her bones.

Shaking her head, she swallowed hard before she spoke.

"Tell me about your family, Elios. Do you have siblings? A wife? Children?"

The corner of his mouth lifted again. "A wife? No, I do not have a wife. Or children. I travel too much to create attachments. I do have a sister, though. Her name is Angelia."

She let out a breath. There was no other woman. The realization filled the hole in her chest ever so slightly until her internal monologue reminded her that he hadn't taken the chance to kiss her. And he was too busy for attachments. She hadn't missed that comment, yet she wished she had.

"Why do you travel so much?"

His face grew serious, and she wondered if it was because of the answer, or because of their circumstance.

"I travel because it's better than being back home. Seeking adventure is a better use of my time at this stage in my life." A chuckle escaped him. "Though I guess I've found quite the adventure with you."

Azure laughed as she used the berries to wash her arms. He tracked her movements just as she had done with him, inching closer.

"Why were you angry earlier? Did I do something wrong?" When she opened her mouth to deny it, he closed the distance between them and lifted her chin with his hand. "And don't tell me you weren't mad. I could tell."

She shrugged, too embarrassed to admit she'd been expecting a kiss, and much too shy to tell him that she wanted anything he would give her. The thought of telling him that she expected to die soon and didn't want to die a virgin filled her with mortification, but it was true. She didn't want to die without ever experiencing a man's touch, even if she would never get to experience the love of one. As though he read her mind, he leaned in. His lips brushed against hers, making the butterflies in her belly take flight. Eyes fluttering shut, she kissed him back.

Chapter Six
STRONGER THAN YOU THINK

E lios' lips on hers sent a shock wave of desire and excitement throughout her body, but the kiss was gentle and much too short, leaving her wanting more. When he pulled away, hands still cradling her face, her chest ached at the absence of him against her lips.

He watched her expression through heavy-lidded eyes, as though he was waiting for her to reject him, but she wouldn't, *she couldn't.* He seemed to realize that quickly, only taking a moment before his lips descended on hers again. Elios' arm snaked around her waist; his earlier restraint gone. Pulling her against his hard body, he tangled his other hand in her still damp hair. She had never kissed anyone before, but it was clear he knew exactly what he was doing. She let him take from her, following his lead as he introduced her to pleasure unlike any she'd ever experienced before.

Elios' touch was somehow both tender and hungry. When he slid his tongue along the seam of her lips, she opened for him, the sensation of his tongue on hers making her belly clench. Her fingers ached to touch him, and though she tried, it was impossible to stifle the desire. Her arms left her sides without conscious thought and wrapped around his muscular body. As her hands traced over the defined planes of his back, she had lost all track of time. When they finally pulled apart, their chests heaved as they panted, desperate for air. Azure felt his arousal pressed against her navel, and it made her nervous, yet excited. Nothing about a man's body was familiar to her, but she needed to learn every inch of his, learn everything that brought him pleasure, even if it was the last thing she did before she died.

"It feels like I've waited forever to do that, even though we've only just met." His blue eyes darkened with passion. They were the color of the sea under the sun's rays, and she couldn't look away.

"I'm relieved you stopped waiting, then. It was better than I'd ever imagined it could be, and I've certainly been imagining."

Elios cocked his head and smirked, his hand making gentle passes along the raised scars of her freshly healed back. She found herself grateful for her accelerated healing, as his touch sent shivers up her spine. "Kissing me?"

Dropping her gaze, a blush staining her cheeks, Azure tucked a lock of hair behind her ear. She knew she needed to come clean about her inexperience eventually, and this seemed like as good a time as any. "Kissing, in general. That was my first time."

Warm fingers traced along her jawline as he gently nudged her chin up and met her eyes. "If it makes you feel any better, I couldn't tell. It was the best kiss I've ever had, and I mean that." His sincere smile made her stomach flutter as the arm around her waist pulled her firmly against him, his face nuzzling into her neck. His hard length twitched between them, punctuating the honesty in his words, and she gasped softly. "I hope you don't mind if I keep doing it."

Her eyes closed as his fingers made another tantalizing sweep along her jaw. "Please." Her whispered plea elicited a gravelly chuckle from him, and when she opened her eyes, she saw a devious glint in his.

"Does that mean you'll let me kiss you again?"

There was barely enough time for her to give a brief nod before his lips were on hers again. His exploration of her mouth was ravenous and thorough, and her body craved more with every passing moment. She was a stranger to sexual touches, aside from those she'd given to herself, but the throbbing between her thighs assured her that her body knew exactly what it wanted. But Elios didn't do any more than kiss her, his hands never drifting beyond her face and back. She couldn't deny her feelings of disappointment, but she didn't know how to initiate more, and she didn't know if she was ready for more.

Something between them had changed in the pool, something that had been brewing since their first touch. When they returned to the fire to dry off, they sat closer than they ever had before. They were nude as they basked in the flames, which made it impossible for Azure not to stare at Elios' magnificent body. She lounged across his lap, the hardness against her thigh telling her just how attracted he was to her, even if he resisted his urges. She had never seen a cock filled with passion before. Her human life had revolved around her little sister, and there was no time for suitors, even if she'd wanted one. Now that a man was in her grasp, she wasn't even sure what to do with him.

Once she'd become a mermaid, Azure had only ever seen human men when she'd led them to their deaths. They were never potential mates. It wouldn't have been allowed, even if she had. Seduction did not go past her ominous song. There were some mermen, but they were all in Miris' inner circle. Any mermaids who lived on the outskirts of Miris' chosen ones were destined to a lonely existence of forced servitude and nothing else.

Azure shook off her morose thoughts, vowing to live in the moment as they cuddled by the fire. Her naked body was pressed against his, and her head was tucked beneath his chin. They didn't move beyond kissing, but their interlaced fingers rested against her thigh, and the hollowness between her legs was undeniable. If he tried to take her, she would let him.

"Where were you headed?"

"Hmm?" Sounding sleepy, Elios placed a gentle kiss on her temple.

"You were on a merchant ship. I assume you paid for passage. I was just curious about your destination."

His face brushed against hers as he rubbed her hand with his thumb. The slight touch set her senses on high. "I was going wherever the wind took me. As long as the ship wasn't returning to Zourin, I didn't care."

"What do you do in unknown places? How do you support yourself?"

She knew she was probably prying too much, but she was too interested to resist. He didn't seem to mind her line of questioning as his thumb continued to stroke hers. She watched the caresses as he answered her endless stream of inquiries, entranced by his tan skin against her pale complexion. She wondered what his sun-kissed flesh would look like moving against hers in the throes of ecstasy. Just the thought of it made her blood boil.

Just as the distraction of his skin began to lure her in, tightness grew in her chest and the guilt returned. She'd ended so many lives, and she hated herself for allowing this glimmer of happiness. It was a terrible time for those thoughts to flood her mind, but she couldn't stop them.

"I'm sorry." Her voice was low, like she didn't want him to hear her, but the kiss he placed on her cheek told her that he had. His life sounded so fascinating, and she ruined it as she had so many others. He may still draw breath, at that moment, but nothing would ever be the same, and she was to blame.

"For what? If you hadn't crashed the ship, another would have." His arm tightened around her waist, lending support when she thought she just may unravel. "I know the guilt must eat away at you, but you didn't have a choice but to do the things you've done. Not by the looks of the scars on your back."

A sour taste rose in her throat, one she knew well. She tried to swallow it down, but it persisted.

"I did have a choice. I still do. I could die, and my life debt would die with me."

Elios' muscled arm tensed, and his fingers wrapped firmly around her hip as he twisted her to face him. His pinched eyebrows created a serious expression she'd never seen on his face before. "Please don't talk like that, Azure. The Sea Goddess will continue her monstrous behavior, with or without you. You dying doesn't change anything but take you away from me."

His care for her filled her heart like a glass of the sweetest wine, and she knew he was right, but her life was *not* worth the thousands her freedom would cost. With every mark she etched on that wall, her life became more worthless. The world would be a better place if she were put down, like any other dangerous animal, but she kept those thoughts to herself, not wanting to upset him more.

"Instead of thinking about removing yourself from the equation, why not find a way to remove her? That's the only way to truly save lives. Surely, there must be a way to defeat her."

Azure huffed a cynical laugh and stared at him, incredulity coating her expression. "She's a goddess. She's untouchable. If there is a power that can destroy her, I don't have it. I'm not sure if anyone does. Not to mention, whoever kills her must take her place. That's not a position I would ever want."

Elios pressed his forehead to hers, forcing her to look into his eyes. "I don't want you to take her place either, but don't give up on her destruction just yet. You're stronger than you think, and I'll help you however I can."

She nodded along, but she didn't agree. She didn't feel strong at all. She was weak—a woman who killed because she wasn't brave enough to die.

The conversation ended their cuddling, and they both rose to pull their clothes back on. Although her body still craved him, she wasn't mentally prepared to go any further. She knew that. The emotional rollercoaster she was on made it impossible. Elios, to her relief, seemed happy to move at whatever pace she was comfortable with. She was drawn to him on a deeper level than she thought was possible. If they lived in a perfect world, they may have still clung to each other just as quickly, but she tried to convince herself that their circumstances played a factor in the speed of their intimacy. It surely couldn't be because her heart was already attached to him. Neither her emotions, nor her mind, believed the lie, but she clung to it as they tended the fire and settled down for bed. They snuggled under the blanket together, their tangled bodies sharing warmth, as she pondered their future, or their lack of one.

Elios' plea for her life continued to ring in Azure's head, but she could not deny that the option was still on the table. She would never see her life as greater than, or even equal to, five thousand others. For the time being, she had an additional reason to live, and that was to ensure his survival, but after that, nothing was guaranteed. She intended to rebel against her curse until there was no other choice, and then only death would end her misery.

Exhaustion weighed down her limbs, giving her the sensation of sinking into the fern fronds they'd used to cushion the stone floor. Elios' arm settled around her waist while he cradled her against his chest. His comforting embrace grounded her, making her feel safer. Brushing the hair away from her eyes, he placed a gentle kiss on her cheek.

"What are you thinking about?" Propped up on an elbow, Elios ran a hand along her side. It felt so good to be touched with so much affection, with so much care.

"Everything and nothing. Today was too easy, and tomorrow is not promised." She rolled onto her back and looked up into his piercing eyes. "What if they're watching and waiting for us to show ourselves?"

His hand trailed from her hip to her stomach, making it hard for her to concentrate.

"We can't fight a battle that doesn't exist. If they are watching us, then it's too late to run, anyway. We have to deal with problems as they come." Elios' warm fingers drew idle patterns over her flat stomach, and she wished he would turn his attention downward if only once. She wanted to put all her reservations aside and give in to temptation. It would have certainly taken her mind off of the inevitable. "All we can do is survive, Azure. Worrying serves no purpose."

She nodded and cupped the back of his head, pulling him into a kiss. His face was strong, so handsomely masculine, but his lips were pillow soft. She considered his words. Worrying only created more stress and achieved little else. He was right, of course. Still, she couldn't smother her endless fears.

"So, we just prepare? Make weapons and train?"

He nodded and kissed her again. Leaning up to deepen the kiss, her fingers glided through his silky hair. The flicker of firelight behind him gave him the appearance of a god sent to tempt her. Her body tingled as he wrapped his arm firmly around her waist and pulled her even closer to his warmth, his teeth digging into her lower lip, eliciting a moan. She wondered if she should—could—throw all caution to the wind. The hardness against her hip assured that his body was ready to claim her. It practically called to her, and the throb between her legs wanted to answer.

A noise sounded from the front chamber of the cave, forcing them apart. Without another word, they listened carefully. Azure's breath came in short bursts as she waited for the sound to repeat itself. She strained her ears, the rapid thrum of her heart making it difficult to hear. Silence lingered for a few moments before they heard the sound again.

The pair jolted upright; the blanket thrown haphazardly aside. Grabbing the dagger beside her, Azure unsheathed the weapon as a slight dragging sound filled the room, followed by something clattering to the ground. Behind her, Elios rose from a crouched position, having banked the fire before quietly arming himself with his sword and a handmade knife. He crept toward the entrance of their chamber without so much as a tap against the stone floor, Azure following closely behind.

The weapons in hand were the only protection they had from whoever intruded upon their sanctuary, but they pushed forward, ready to meet their enemy head on. Tiptoeing in the darkness, the couple made their way down the narrow corridor toward the front chamber.

Another object thudded to the ground, echoing through the cramped space. It was likely one of the stones that blocked the cave entrance, but they couldn't be sure. They peered through the small opening that looked into the large room, but although there were gaps in the stones blocking the entrance, the light of the moon did little to illuminate the space. Azure grabbed onto the waistband of Elios' trousers, more to comfort herself than for guidance. He reached back and squeezed her hand before continuing forward.

The cave felt too small, the air too thin. In the moon's faint glow, they watched another stone that blocked the entrance tumble to the floor. Whoever was trying to get in was deliberately knocking their way through the barricade. Tension radiated from Elios, and it made Azure nervous as she squinted toward the blockage that served as their final defense. Hopefully, whatever it was would give up and walk away. At least, that was Azure's hope, undoubtedly a foolish one.

An animalistic growl filled the space before the sound of loud footsteps retreated, fading into the distance. Elios leaned in until his lips nearly touched her face.

"It was just an animal, and it seems to have given up." His words were punctuated by a gentle nip on her ear.

"Any idea what kind?"

Grabbing her arm gently, he led her back to their chamber and settled before the fire, pulling her onto his lap. "I'm not sure what types of animals are native to this island. Perhaps we can find clues to its identity in the morning. It's too dark to see anything right now, anyway."

Azure nodded, alert tension giving way to exhaustion as she relaxed.

The late-night intruder had been a bucket of ice water on what was sure to be a steamy night. Their desire was put on hold, but when they retired for the night, they slept close. Elios cradled her to his chest, his muscular arm protectively coiled around her waist. Their noisy barrier at the entrance had proven to be an effective deterrent for unwanted animal guests, but she hoped it would have the same effect on those who hunted them.

Her worries warred against her need for sleep, but eventually the warmth of Elios' embrace lulled her busy mind, and oblivion consumed her.

*W*aves crashed against the shore, washing away the sand beneath Daneliya's unmoving feet as her body slowly turned a sickening gray. Azure's shoulders shook with the force of her sobs, a torrent of emotions she couldn't stop. Her little sister was dead, and it was her fault. Her one role in life was to protect the child, and she'd failed so tragically. There was no coming back from such a costly mistake.

Scanning the desolate beach around them, she tried to scream for help, but no sound left her lips. Her voiceless screams and soundless sobs were swallowed by the darkness that encompassed the landscape.

Sitting up and cupping the little girl's face, Azure stroked her cold, clammy cheek with her thumb as she silently begged for life to return to her little sister's features. She clung to Daneliya's lifeless body, desperately hoping someone would come to save her, but knowing no one would. No one could. It was too late.

As though her wish were being granted, the seven-year-old's eyes snapped open, but her irises were pitch black, the obsidian stare locking on Azure, turning her blood to ice. It wasn't her wish at all. She was the older sister, the protector, but fear and disgust at the grotesque thing looking through her sister's eyes ravaged in her stomach as the midnight glare held her in place. She wanted to shove the child aside and run, but her arms wouldn't let go.

Her stomach wretched, nothing coming up but salty water, as Daneliya's tiny blue lips parted, and words came out in an eerie hiss that sent terror racing through Azure's body. "She's coming. She'll find you. You will never be safe."

Even in her dream, all Azure could do was scream.

CHAPTER SEVEN
THE ATTACK

F ive more days passed in the same manner as the first few did. Azure and Elios spent most of their time crafting weapons, training, or wrapped in each other's arms. Although Azure's body pulsed with the need for more, the stress of their situation kept them from moving any further. They kissed and teased, grinding their bodies against each other's, but there was always a layer of clothing separating them. The unspoken promise of more was yet to be fulfilled.

After more than a week had passed, Azure finally felt safe enough to reenter the water. They'd run out of dried fish, and though the island provided plenty of fruit, it wasn't enough. So, when she awoke on the eighth day, she slipped out of bed and left the cave as quietly as possible, aiming for the beach.

Dark clouds loomed over the horizon as day broke overhead, threatening an intense thunderstorm. The winds rolling off the sea held a chill that prickled Azure's skin as she crossed the deserted beach. Even armed with a handmade spear and Elios' dagger, she still felt vulnerable. She was beginning to regret her decision to not wake him as she slid into the rough waters and shifted her into her mermaid form.

Azure scanned her surroundings for any sign of a ship or another mermaid, but she saw none as she hovered near the tenuous safety the shore offered. A flock of white birds flew overhead, fleeing the incoming storm and bringing with them an ominous sign of things to come. She treaded water as she watched them disappear into the distance. Letting out a deep breath, Azure tucked the dagger into her roughly fashioned leather belt and gripped the primitive spear before ducking below the surface.

Although her cursed vision allowed her to see clearly underwater, the turbulence of the waves made it challenging. The storm was still far out, but the current was already being affected. To increase visibility, she ventured further out, escaping the waves as they crashed against the shore. She dove deep until she neared the sea floor, where a world of life waited for her to claim its bounties.

The colorful creatures and coral were always breathtaking, but she didn't enjoy seeing them anymore. Her curse gave her negative feelings about the water, and though she once marveled at the sights the sea held, its unyielding beauty was now a punishment. She didn't deserve to enjoy such things when she led so many men to this watery grave.

She ignored the visuals, moving her tail slowly to avoid scaring the fish, and inched toward the underwater foliage that held the promise of a meal. The plants swayed in the current, giving sanctuary to several types of fish. It would hide them from most predators, but not from her.

Thrusting the spear forward, she impaled two fish on its stone tip before they had the instinct to swim away. She reveled in her success as she killed the fish, ending their suffering, excited at the prospect of bringing Elios fresh meat for dinner. Imagining his surprise and joy at the size of her catch made her smile.

A dark shadow moved overhead, drawing Azure's attention from her thoughts. Her surroundings chilled as she tried to swallow her growing anxiety, no longer feeling safe in the water. Tucking her catch into the pouch that hung from her belt, she moved toward the surface.

Rain assaulted her as she took her first breath of air, making it difficult to see the island in the distance. Panic hitting her, she scanned the surface of the water but couldn't find the source of the shadow. She headed for the shore, hoping the darkness was nothing more than a figment of her imagination, or a large fish, but as she neared the beach, her heart ripped open at what she saw.

Through the thick sheet of rain, Azure spotted Elios in his fighting stance, sword in hand, as he glared at the two women opposite him. *Oona and Lucia.* Her stomach clenched, her heart beating so hard it made her lightheaded as she moved closer. The desire to race toward him, to help in any way she could, was overwhelming, but she wasn't a skilled warrior. The element of surprise was the only thing on her side, and she couldn't afford to lose it.

She strained her ears to hear them above the crashing waves and rolling thunder, but the view became clearer as she stealthily approached. Holding her hands out, Oona threatened to unleash her powers if Elios didn't tell her where his savior was. Lucia sneered at him over the dagger she clutched, but Elios was unyielding. He wouldn't betray her.

"I've already told you. I don't know who she is. I'm here alone."

Elios' firm voice carried. He was protecting her. Bile rose in Azure's throat at the realization. She was supposed to keep him safe, not the other way around.

"Lies!" Oona spat, scanning the island for some sign of her prey.

Azure's eyes were barely above the surface as she moved forward, still not knowing how to turn the tides of the ambush. If Oona took only moments to concentrate, she could have squeezed the air from Elios' lungs with the twist of her hand, unless Miris had ordered her bounty hunters to bring them back alive. After spending decades as Miris' most loyal servant, she'd developed powers that Azure could only dream of. Oona was just as evil as her mistress.

Aside from strength, endurance, and impeccable sight, Azure had no other otherworldly abilities. Well, those along with her haunting, sultry song, but all mermaids had such skills. There was something more wicked in Oona, more than just her love for killing, something Azure couldn't comprehend.

While Elios had their attention, Azure shifted and slipped onto the bank, sneaking into the tree line unnoticed. She wished she could give him a signal that she was there, and hadn't abandoned him, but there was no way to do that without giving away her location. She had to remain hidden to plan her attack, although her mind was too chaotic for plans, just as they'd been on the night she had pulled him from the water.

Over the last several days, she and Elios had hidden weapons throughout the island, just in case they were ever cornered, like they were at this moment. There were not many, but Azure found the makeshift dagger nearest to her in no time. She still had Elios' dagger and the spear, but she didn't want to use those just yet. If things progressed to hand-to-hand contact, she may have needed them. Something she prayed wouldn't happen. She had no confidence in her ability to fight with her hands, especially against such vicious enemies. Silent as a wraith, she aimed the blade and threw as Oona spat another threat at Elios.

A high-pitched scream broke the droning of the storm. Azure watched as her target fell to the ground, clutching at her right shoulder that the makeshift dagger was now buried in. It was embedded just below her shoulder blade, making the mermaid's arms less lethal, for at least a moment.

The blood-thirsty mermaid scanned the trees, searching for her attacker, but Azure was hidden within the dense brush. Using the distraction to his advantage, Elios charged Lucia, thrusting out his sword and knocking her dagger from her grasp. She growled as he scooped up the weapon before she had the chance.

"I'm going to get you for that, human," Lucia snarled as she darted over and yanked the blade from Oona's shoulder. The mermaid still held her arm, hissing as blood poured down her back.

With obvious difficulty, Oona stood and tried to lift her hands toward the sky. She was in pain, though the wound would heal quickly, and it showed. Elios and Lucia circled each other, preparing for a fight that Elios would not necessarily win, no matter how trained he was. Azure needed to plan her next move carefully, or he wouldn't stand a chance. There was never a reason for her to prepare for such a thing before, but even with her shortcomings, she would die to save him. Oona's power was too great, and Lucia was ruthless. They would stop at nothing to get to her, and a human would not stop them. In their eyes, his soul already belonged to Miris, anyway.

The clanging of blades, accompanied by grunts, pulled Azure's attention from Oona's struggle. Lucia's legs were wrapped around Elios, as their arms wrestled for purchase against the other. Both of their blades were abandoned on the ground. Lucia was smaller and didn't have powers like her friend, but the mermaid was still abnormally strong, like a rabid dog. Elios didn't have the upper hand, strength-wise, even with his larger, muscled build.

Azure's heartbeat was erratic as adrenaline surged through her veins. She needed to do something—anything. Wrapping a trembling hand around the hilt of Elios' dagger, she took aim and hurled the blade. The weapon cut through the air like an arrow but missed its target. Oona ducked, the blade narrowly overshooting her head. The mermaid drew her own knife and spun toward the trees. Squeezing her eyes shut for a moment, Azure tried to calm the rapid breathing that caused spots in her vision.

Behind Oona, Lucia restrained Elios beneath her as they both struggled to reach the blades that rested less than a few feet away. Her blond hair was a matted mess hanging on his face.

"I know you're there, Azure." Oona's disdain and sheer cockiness laced her words. She smirked in Azure's direction, although she didn't seem to see her in the dense foliage. The struggle behind the mermaid stopped as Lucia managed to get a hand on the bloody dagger she'd pulled from her companion's shoulder and pressed it against Elios' throat. Azure's muscles tensed as tight as bowstrings as she gripped her primitive spear so tight the wood groaned.

"Show yourself, or we'll kill your lover boy." Oona glanced over her healing shoulder at Elios pinned beneath her friend. Azure took a ragged breath. "Not that we won't kill him, anyway. I mean." Oona chuckled. "He's basically already a dead man."

Lucia laughed and spit on the ground beside Elios' head. He thrashed his legs, trying to force the violent mermaid off him, to no avail. She pressed the blade firmer into his throat but didn't draw blood. *Yet.* Azure fought back the urge to cry out as she watched Elios go slack beneath his attacker. She was out of options.

Drawing in a shaky breath, Azure stepped out of her hiding place. "If I surrender, you have to let him go."

Oona looked bored as she used the tip of her blade to clean her fingernails. "I don't know, Azure. Our Goddess would be quite angry if we set him free. His soul belongs to her."

Azure's heart drummed in her ears, harmonizing with the rain hitting the surrounding ground. "He belongs to no one! He's a free man—an innocent." Rage clouded her vision as she fought to still her trembling hands. "And she is NOT my Goddess!"

Oona tsked, glancing behind herself again. "Kil-" Before she could finish her command, giant tentacles thrust out of the raging sea, grabbing the snarling mermaid and pulling her beneath the surface. Azure took a step forward but halted as Lucia's head snapped to where the unknown creature had disappeared with her companion.

"Oona!" Lucia screamed, pushing away from Elios and darting for the water. She shifted midair as she dove in after her friend, disappearing beneath the crashing waves.

Staring in stunned silence, neither Azure nor Elios spoke. Azure waited, certain the massive creature would resurface and take them both, but there was no sign of the monster. *It was gone.* Icy fear spread through her body as she recalled the beast. It was the stuff of legends, a creature that was never meant to exist. *The Kraken.*

Warm arms wrapped around her as she fixated on the dark water, trying to understand what had just happened. Elios squeezed her tightly, peppering her with kisses.

"Are you okay?" His words were breathless as he pulled away, scanning her face. "You were amazing."

Her gaze remained on the sea and the now empty space where the creature had been only a moment before. "What was that?" She asked, but she already knew the answer.

Elios pulled her close, tucking her head below his chin as he stroked her back. "I've heard stories of such a monster before. Sailors love to tell tales of the Kraken, but I never believed they were true."

Closing her eyes, she allowed the warmth of Elios' touch to chase away the chill of the terror that consumed her.

"Come," Elios said as he wrapped his arm around her shoulders and began guiding her back to the cave. "Let's go sit by the fire and warm up. You're shivering."

She knew her trembles were from the day's events rather than the temperature, but she let Elios lead her back inside.

Chapter Eight
PERFECT

The fire was nearly extinguished when they returned to the back chamber of the cavern, but Elios rekindled the flames easily. As soon as the blaze was stable, he sat in front of it and pulled Azure into his lap. She nuzzled against him.

"Who were they? Did you know those mermaids?"

Azure nodded, grimacing. "Unfortunately. Though, I wish I didn't. The one you fought was Lucia. She's damn near feral, prefers to kill with her hands over singing. The one I hit with the dagger was Oona. Her magic is dangerous. She could've killed you with a wave of her hand if she'd wanted to." Saying it out loud only made her stomach churn more. "Miris must have ordered them to bring us to her alive. They would have killed us with no hesitation otherwise."

Shuddering, she thought about the future that would have awaited them if not for the giant, tentacled creature that had miraculously come to their rescue. The sadistic torture they would have faced at Miris' hand if they hadn't been saved plagued her thoughts. The Kraken bought them some time, but not much. They needed to leave the island *soon*.

Elios tucked a strand of hair behind her ear. "Well, I don't think Oona will come back from that. Lucia, I'm not so sure."

He ran his fingers up and down her spine, sending tingles all over her body. Closing her eyes, she luxuriated in the feeling, trying not to focus on the worries that threatened to consume her.

"I was so scared something would happen to you. I'm sorry I didn't wake you before I went fishing. I wanted to let you rest. It was stupid."

Twisting her toward him, Elios' soft lips touched hers in a gentle caress. Even in such a tumultuous moment, even after he'd fought for his life, he was so tender. "You have nothing to apologize for. You couldn't have known they were watching us."

He was right, but she wouldn't make the same mistake again. They needed to stay together. It was them, against the world. Wrapping her arms around his neck, Azure pulled him closer, and deepened the kiss as her hand slid into his silky brown hair. She'd never needed a distraction so much in her life.

She could have lost him, and that realization added an urgency to every stroke of her tongue. They weren't guaranteed tomorrow. That moment was the only thing they were promised. They should be trapped in a dungeon, or dead, but they'd survived.

A legendary creature had erupted from the sea and saved them. None of it was a coincidence, and Azure was certain that fate was on their side, at least for the moment. They were meant to be together. That was what she told herself as his mouth descended on her neck, and she threw back her head in bliss. She would no longer waste time denying what she wanted, what they both wanted. Desire consumed their kisses, and she was ready to give in to those wants before the chance was lost.

A groan escaped him as she turned, straddling his lap. The limited amount of clothing separating their bodies was scandalous, but she didn't care. If anything, it fueled her. It was her first time in such a position with a man, with his throbbing length settled against her center, but with Elios, the moment was special. She would give herself to him until she no longer had breath in her lungs and would cherish every second they had together.

Their kisses grew ravenous as Elios slid his hands down her back and gripped her backside, his strong fingers kneading into her flesh. Anticipation charged the air, and her breaths came quicker as she rolled her hips, grinding against the hardness beneath her.

She needed more. Her body all but begged for it. Every inch of her was on the verge of combusting, and the fire within her needed to be stoked. He seemed to sense her need. Elios' rough grip moved to her hips, pulling her against him, dragging her sex along his entire length. She hissed as a strike of electricity shot through her center, making her need frantic. The foreign sensation wound her tighter, and she needed release before she exploded.

"We don't have to go any further," he said against her neck, his voice deep and full of unquenched need. The feel of his warm breath against her skin intensified the sensitivity she already felt. Her entire frame strummed with life against him.

Fingers biting into his firm back, she nuzzled his neck and nipped at his flesh before responding. "I don't want to stop." She didn't know what to expect, or even what to do, but she wanted him anyway. She wanted to experience all of him before she lost the opportunity for something good in her life, one moment of bliss in a sea of hurt.

Elios groaned, the sound full of promise, as he stood and carried her to their makeshift bed, setting her down and covering her body with his. It was nothing more than foliage and leather blankets, but the bedding felt luxurious as he stared into her eyes. Before she could move, his mouth was on hers again, hungry and punishing. It was more than just a kiss between them. The emotions that filled it penetrated her hardened heart and connected them on a level she didn't understand. She was to be his, and he was hers, until their hearts stopped beating.

Azure moaned as his tongue moved against hers in the most tantalizing of dances. His deft fingers made quick work of the knot that secured her leather top. His movements were frantic, as if he didn't free her body at that second, she would disappear from under him. The second he released her breasts, he tossed the fabric to the floor, never looking away from her.

In the dim firelight, Azure watched as Elios' brilliant blue eyes darkened, lust filling his stare as he fixated on her chest. It wasn't the first time he'd seen her topless, but this was different. Her breasts were rather small, nothing special, but the way he licked his lips made her feel like the most beautiful woman in the world.

Every time he'd seen her exposed before, it was out of necessity. This time, her nudity came with an invitation for him to touch her. Still, his eyes met hers with a silent question, waiting for her permission to move forward. Grabbing his hand, Azure placed a kiss on his palm before setting it against her skin. Whatever had paralyzed him before vanished.

Elios lurched forward, his mouth on hers as he gently squeezed her breast, rubbing his thumb over the taut point. She arched into his touch as she throbbed between her legs, aching to be filled. He settled a thigh between her legs as his hands explored her torso, fingers digging into her waist and skimming her stomach. Writhing beneath him, she groaned, the sound coming from deep within her chest.

Smiling against her lips at her obvious need, he trailed kisses across her neck before nipping at her ear. She never knew ears could be so sensitive, but as he bit the shell, running his tongue along it, she was driven wild with lust. Her hands itched to touch him. She slid them along his back, feeling the muscles ripple as he hovered over her and explored her body with his mouth. His tongue lashed at her breasts before he pulled a nipple into the warmth of his mouth.

"Elios." She panted, lifting her head to watch his ministrations. The next tug of his teeth sent a surge of pleasure through her, forcing her head back against the bedding. For this moment, on this night, she pushed the fear and worry out of her mind, allowing herself to revel in passion for the first time in her life.

"I want to kiss all of you, Azure." His voice was low, a sensual whisper against her chest.

"Please." It was the only thing she could say, a deep yearning thickening her tone. The sultry sound that fell from her lips surprised her, but she didn't have time to dwell on it. She held her breath as she watched his wicked mouth journey from her chest to her stomach.

"You are so beautiful... *Perfect.*"

Her chest heaved with every breath as Elios slid his tongue across her stomach, while his hands roamed down to her hips and to her thighs. The throbbing between her legs grew more insistent the lower his lips moved, and she found it impossible to stay still as his hands continued to explore her.

The moment Miris had stripped her of her freedom, her humanity, Azure thought she'd lost the chance to experience what it meant to be loved by a man. Maybe, if she had stayed human, she could've found a man to love and marry her. But, since being turned into a monster—the slave of a greater evil—love and passion became something she no longer believed was in the cards for her. Until she saved Elios. He changed everything, and she was beginning to think he was the one who saved her, not the other way around.

Elios' tongue circled her navel, so close to where she wanted him. It was maddening, and her hips rolled beneath him in a silent plea for him to move his teasing mouth lower. She didn't need experience to understand the need that coursed through her. Learning enough through idle conversations with other females, she knew his mouth could relieve the ache. She just didn't know how to ask for it but hoped he would understand her uncontrolled movements enough to discern what her body was begging for.

As though he had a direct link to her mind, Elios inched his large body down hers, settling between her legs. Warm breath caressed the apex of her thighs and her breath hitched. All that separated his mouth from her flesh was the leather of her loin-cloth. She bit her lip with anticipation as he hooked one of her legs over his shoulder.

"Do you want me to stop? We can stop at any time." His voice was a low, rumbling whisper, the vibration of it tingling against her skin.

She appreciated the offer but shook her head vehemently as she fumbled with the knots of the cursed garment that stood in her way of the promise of ecstasy. "Please don't stop." Her voice was breathy—desperate.

She'd never come across a more ridiculously infuriating knot in her life, even if she was the one who had created it. Elios chuckled as he swatted her hand away and untangled the clasp of her bottoms, sliding the leather cloth off and throwing it over his shoulder. She watched as he stared unblinking at her bare sex, as if he were a starving man given his first meal. Her body throbbed, but instead of soothing her desperate need, Elios placed a kiss on her thigh, continuing the trail down her leg and completely neglecting where she really wanted him.

"You are so cruel."

His resounding grunt sounded a bit too much like a chuckle as he placed a kiss on the crook of her knee. "You don't really think I'm cruel, Azure. If there's something you want, all you need to do is ask."

Her eyes rolled in her head, her hips bucking as his tongue trailed up the inside of her thigh. She didn't know the words to ask. Groaning with needy frustration, she grabbed the back of his head and brought his face to her center. To her relief, he obliged, his grin pure wickedness as he nestled between her legs. She couldn't look away as the first graze of his tongue traced through her folds, setting her body ablaze. She moaned, closing her eyes and throwing her head back as she fisted the ferns beneath her. A groan rumbled deep in his chest, as if he'd just tasted the most delicious of cakes. He stroked her sensitive bundle of nerves with bruising kisses, sending her pleasure in waves. Nothing had ever felt so divine.

Flattening one hand against her belly, holding her in place, Elios used the other to grip her thigh, keeping her open for him. She grabbed the back of his head, tangling her fingers in his hair, pushing him closer. Only responding with another groan, he increased the pressure of his skilled ministrations as he devoured her. She felt like a spring that was wound so tight she'd break. She moaned and thrashed, squeezing his head between her legs as he worked the bundle of nerves, filling her with desperate need, making her all too aware of the void in her that needed filling.

"Oh, gods. Elios." She panted, so close to erupting she could practically taste it. Just when she thought it couldn't possibly feel any more consuming, he slid his large fingers inside of her and worked her body from the inside and out. Her insides squeezed around him, the coil winding tighter until she shattered.

Azure screamed with the force of her orgasm. The euphoric waves crashed over her as he continued to worship her body with his mouth and his hands. His groan of approval only increased the pleasure in her lust-addled state as her thighs clenched around his face. He wrung every bit of bliss out of her, leaving her breathless. Her chest heaved, her head weak and weightless.

She was in a daze. Her body felt like nothing more than jelly. Elios placed one more lingering kiss on the inside of her thigh before sliding his body up against hers, like a predator stalking his prey. She watched him, mesmerized. His cerulean eyes heated into the color of the deep sea as he watched her, filled with a hunger she'd never seen before.

His muscles were taut, his body primed to take all of her, if she was willing to give it to him. He leaned forward and kissed her again, his chest heaving as much as hers. The taste she'd become so familiar with was mixed with her own, and the thought made her want him even more. Just thinking about what he had just done to her was enough to rebuild the tension in her body that her climax had just loosened. No one had ever made her feel like that before.

"We don't have to go further if you're not ready." He kept offering her an out, but she had no intention of taking it. Nothing would keep her from letting him claim her. *Nothing.* Wrapping her legs around his waist, she could feel just how much he wanted her. He hissed as she ground against him, his eyes closing as she rubbed her center against his rock-hard length, covering his trousers in her release.

"I want all of you. I want everything." She dragged her nails up his back, just enough to make it sting. "I need you."

When he leaned in to kiss her again, their teeth clashed with the intensity of it. He was so close, and suddenly the fabric of his trousers irritated her. Without them, it would only take a small movement, and they would be joined as one. She pushed him away, hands desperate to remove his only shred of clothing. As soon as he returned to her, her legs went around him once again, and she squeezed. Her center slid along his hardness, the proof of her orgasm slicking his skin, moaning at the friction of his bare flesh against hers.

"I'm on a preventative, Azure." Elios' voice was labored, like he couldn't wait any longer to claim her, but he needed her to know this.

"What's that?" Not knowing, or caring, what a preventative was, she panted. She just wanted him. *Now.*

"Preventative. It prevents pregnancy."

Before that moment, pregnancy had not been on her mind. She didn't even know if mermaids could get pregnant, but she nodded, pulling his mouth to hers as she lifted her hips to grind against his cock once more. She was tired of waiting.

His tenuous hold on his restraint broke, and he angled himself at her channel, pushing into her, but only slightly. He watched her expression. She knew he was afraid to hurt her, but she didn't have the same reservations. She'd never had sex, and Elios seemed... big, but she had no experience to know what to expect. Even with him not being fully sheathed, he filled her so completely, but the pain was tinged with the sweetest pleasure, and she wanted more. His arms shook as he held himself back, moving ever so slowly as he slid his length into her, waiting for her body to acclimate to his size. She wanted him to let go, to take everything she had to give, but the buildup was delicious.

Lifting her hips to meet his, Azure wrapped her legs tighter around his waist, and he thrusted in a little farther. "Are you okay? Am I hurting you?" His forehead leaned against hers as his blazing eyes bore into her, his breathing rough and shallow.

Shaking her head as she squeezed him tighter, she pressed her swollen lips against his, her tongue sliding into his mouth. It was all the convincing he needed to bury himself fully inside her. She gasped, digging her nails into the straining muscles of his arms. The feeling of his heated skin against hers, the scent of his sweat filling her nose, threatened to shatter her mind. The roll of his hips brought her closer to the brink of climax with every thrust. He felt incredible inside her, and the noises he made sent her deeper into a lust-filled haze. As the coil wound in her belly again, their bodies lost their steady rhythm and moved in a desperate frenzy as they chased their release. This time, when Azure crested over the edge, Elios went with her.

Chapter Nine
GETTING TO SAFETY

I *mages flashed by at a dizzying speed, warbling like reflections on the water just before a rainstorm.*

Miris seated in front of a fire, flipping fervently through papers before tossing them into the flames.

Azure smelled the smoke as they burned.

Flash.

Ocevia tucked away in an undersea cave, peering between the rocks into the dark abyss beyond.

Flash.

The vision swirled, pinching and warping until her friend disappeared. The rapid barrage flickering between scenes, faster and faster, until it was impossible to make out what she was seeing at all.

Without warning, the images halted and settled on the beach, the same beach where everything went wrong. The lens narrowed, fo-

cusing in on Daneliya. Azure's little sister skipped along the sand, giggling, and reaching out to touch the waves that rolled in as the tide licked at her ankles. The child's smile fell as she faded away.

"Daneliya! Wait!" Azure knew what would happen next. The current would sweep her sister out to sea, and the violent waves would steal the breath from her lungs. Visions of blue flesh and an unmoving chest were blades to Azure's stomach as she struggled to break free from the spot she was rooted in, but she couldn't move. She could only watch as history repeated itself. Sobs shook her entire body as she watched the scene fold in on itself, disappearing into nothing.

"Wait."

T he sound of stone hitting stone roused Azure from her sleep. She was still in Elios' arms, cheeks wet from the tears in her dream. She swiped at the tears as her ears strained to listen. Her lover didn't stir at the noise, and she began to wonder if she'd imagined it. After their encounter with Oona and Lucia, she didn't want to risk ignoring it.

Sitting upright, she reached for Elios' dagger before shaking him awake. Maybe it was another animal, maybe it was nothing at all, but they needed to check. Dazed from sleep, he was rubbing his eyes when another crash sounded from the cave's entrance. A human groan followed the noise, and her lover surged to his feet, grabbing his sword without hesitation.

Creeping past the screen separating their chamber from the other, Elios led the way toward the intruder. He held his finger to his mouth as he peered around the corner and into the darkened front chamber. Unable to resist looking, Azure ducked under his arm and peaked into the blackness as well.

The room was too dark to see anything more than a shadowed body lying on the floor in a heap. The sun had already set, and the moon was only a tiny sliver. They couldn't see much, but whoever had broken into the cave seemed to be injured. Azure knew it could be a trap, but curiosity burned in her gut. As she fought the desire to get closer, another groan broke the silence.

"Azure?" The voice was muffled, but unmistakable. "Azure, are you still there?"

Pushing past Elios, Azure darted into the main chamber, falling to her knees beside the wounded figure.

Naked and curled into a fetal position, Ocevia was certainly hurt, but as Azure scanned her body in the darkness, she couldn't tell where the blood was stemming from. She took a deep breath, trying to calm herself, before slowing her inspection, taking care to notice every detail. Blood pooled beneath her friend, but the source appeared to be under her. Ocevia groaned, trying to climb to her feet, only to collapse.

"Elios... Come help her. Let's get her back to the fire."

Elios approached, his expression wary as he scooped Ocevia up in his arms and brought her to the room in the back of the cave. As soon as he set her friend down beside the pool, Azure began assessing the injuries again. The mermaid's eyes fluttered as she fought to stay conscious. Panic surged within Azure, but she pushed it aside. She would have time to lose her mind later. At that moment, she had to stop the bleeding.

"What happened to you, Ocevia?" She applied pressure to a deep gash on Ocevia's thigh while looking for other injuries. Her friend tried to speak, but a pain-filled moan was all she managed to get out.

"I need something to staunch the bleeding," Azure snapped at Elios, fear leaking into her voice. He rushed over to the clothes that were strewn across the floor. They had fallen asleep naked after their passion-filled night and had not paused to dress when they heard Ocevia breaking in. They were still naked, although Elios grabbed his trousers while gathering cloth to wrap the wound.

Ripping the sleeve from his tunic, he returned and wrapped the cloth tightly around Ocevia's leg, tying it off and applying pressure to the wound. Azure used the rest of his tunic to wash away the blood that coated her friend's skin, murmuring soothing words to calm her. When she found no other injuries, the pair watched the wound continue to seep under the force of Elios' hands and prayed it would clot quickly.

Azure rinsed her red-stained skin and added more wood to the fire. Trading places with Elios, she applied pressure to Ocevia's thigh, before asking him to set her friend beside the flames. She wanted to know what happened, who did this to her, but Ocevia was in no condition to explain. All they could do was wait for her to wake up and hope the wound didn't get infected.

Thankfully, Ocevia's wound clotted after a few more minutes. A human would not have survived such a fatal blow to their arteries, but mermaids healed faster. Once Ocevia was safe from bleeding out, Azure and Elios left her to rest and went to wash off.

"Do you trust her?" Elios asked as he approached Azure, wrapping his arms around her waist. She sunk deeper into the warm water and pressed her cheek to his chest, letting the steady beat of his heart calm her nerves.

"With my life... She's my best friend."

Elios cradled her close as he leaned against the rocky side of the pool.

"Was she able to tell you what happened? I mean, before I picked her up."

"Unfortunately, no. She mostly just said my name." An unpleasant thought entered Azure's mind, and she pulled away from his embrace, whipping around to face him as she gasped. "You don't think Oona or Lucia attacked her, do you? Or that creature? Oh gods, Oona couldn't have survived that. Right?"

Elios pulled her back against him and rubbed a gentle hand down her back. "I don't think there is any way Oona survived that creature. As far as the other one, I don't know." His hand stilled on her back for a moment. "If she was injured then, why did it take her so long to find us? I mean, I guess the injury could have slowed her down, but it's been more than half a day since Oona was attacked. The timing is strange."

Azure considered this. It had been a while since the other mermaids entered the sea again, so the timeline made little sense. Ocevia couldn't have been injured in that chaos, but what else could have happened to her? Mermaids were not invincible, but the odds of Ocevia being severely wounded by something else, right after the attack on their island, were too much of a coincidence. But there was no way to know for sure until her friend woke up. All she could do was hope her enemies had not survived the Kraken attack.

Azure's stomach twisted painfully as she tried to fall asleep. Even wrapped up in Elios' arms, her worries would not stop plaguing her. If Miris' people managed to escape the Kraken, there was little doubt they would regroup and return to capture them.

Slipping out of bed, she watched over Ocevia as Elios slept, waiting for her friend to wake up and tell her what happened. They needed to leave the island as soon as Ocevia was well enough to travel. She wouldn't feel safe until they were as far away from the island as they could get. She would even brave the human lands if needed. It no longer mattered that it was forbidden. All that mattered to her was their safety.

She would find a way for her and Ocevia to dip their tails so they wouldn't rot. A tub or maybe even a river, something, but she would do everything in her power to make sure they survived. Going into the human lands did not guarantee safety, because Miris had people everywhere, but there were so many more places to hide among the masses. It gave them a chance, however slim, at survival.

Azure stared at the flickering fire for hours, lost in thought, before the monotony lulled her into a dreamless and fitful slumber. Every time she woke, she feared that the sneering face of Lucia would be hovering over her, but the dim cave was the only thing she saw each time she opened her eyes.

Ocevia groaned, breaking the silence, and Azure's eyes shot open once more. She rushed to her friend's side with a glass of water, but Ocevia was still unconscious. Her friend had rolled onto her back, triggering the painful sound, but hadn't woken up. Setting the glass beside Ocevia, Azure stoked the fire before sitting on the floor next to the make-shift bed where Elios slept.

Every sound from outside startled her, snapping her attention to the screen that blocked their exit. Elios had repositioned the stones and branches at the cave's entrance after Ocevia stabilized, but she was still unnerved and felt incredibly exposed. They had been found twice in one day. The likelihood of someone else knowing their location was higher than she felt comfortable with. Her desperation to flee further away grew by the second.

In the early morning hours, before the sun rose from her slumber, Azure fell back asleep. When she woke again, Elios was awake and checking Ocevia's wound. A leather pouch, full of boiling water, hung over the fire from a tripod they'd previously crafted. Using a strip of cloth, Elios cleaned the wound gently. Ocevia slept soundly, and thankfully the gash in her leg had already begun scabbing over. He glanced over at Azure as she stood, smiling at her.

"How's she doing?" Azure asked as she joined him beside the fire, crouching to take a closer look. The scab was bigger than she'd expected, the entire wound covered by it, but there was no sign of infection.

Elios leaned in and whispered in her ear. "It looks good, but she hasn't woken yet. It's healing faster than I expected."

"One of the few perks of being a mermaid. Fast healing."

He arched an eyebrow as he continued his ministrations, re-wrapping the wound before tucking the blanket around her friend. Taking one more cursory look at Ocevia, Azure and Elios stood and headed for the heated water of the pool so he could clean his hands.

"What's the plan now?" he asked, splashing water on his face. She watched as the droplets danced seductively down the muscles of his bare chest and stomach, swallowing hard as she tried to focus on his question.

When she forced her eyes back to his face, he was grinning at her, and she blushed at being caught admiring his form. She cleared her throat. "Plan for what?" The flush spread across her cheeks, and his grin became more mischievous as he elaborated.

"Plan for what we do next. It's not safe to stay here now that we've been found." He dried his hands on his trousers before wrapping his arms around her and pulling her in close. His scent filled her nose, mingling with hers. Being pressed against his bare skin reminded her of the ways their bodies touched the night before, and warmth spread all the way from her fingers to toes. She pulled away, unable to focus while in his embrace.

"Well, we can't leave until Ocevia can shift and swim. I can't carry both of you. But you're right. I'm not comfortable staying here any longer than we have to."

Nodding, Elios looked toward the cave's opening. "We can make a raft. There's plenty of wood out there. We can use vines and strips of the sail to bind it. If we fashion paddles, neither of you would need to shift or swim."

The thought never occurred to her, but he was on to something. If no one was watching the cave, they couldn't be tracked. When they were in the sea, their scent could be picked up along the current if their pursuers were close enough, but if they never entered the water...

The plan began to form in her mind, and she nodded, explaining the tracking bit to Elios.

"Shall we go collect wood then?"

Azure glanced at the sleeping Ocevia again before grabbing his hand. "Let's do it."

CHAPTER TEN
THE PLAN

C ollecting wood for their raft went quickly. Trying to avoid prying eyes, Azure and Elios searched the forest first before scanning the shore. They were too close to be leaving the island for the human lands to get caught now. With an injured Ocevia, getting as far away from Miris was even more urgent. There were too many lives on the line.

They found a broken section of a ship that washed ashore on the southern end of the island. It was only large enough to fit one person lying down, but it was a lucky find, and would serve as an excellent foundation to build upon.

They worked in the front chamber of the cave, giving them more space and the ability to speak freely without disturbing the sleeping mermaid. Azure checked on her regularly, but by the time the sun peaked in the sky, Ocevia was still asleep.

Whatever happened before she got injured, however far she'd swam, or however hard she fought, must have drained every bit of her energy. They kept an eye on her as they worked on their escape plan, hoping she'd wake in time to leave.

By the time the raft was complete, it was large enough to hold all three of them in the seated position, but the space would be a little tighter if Ocevia needed to lie down, which seemed the likely scenario. Still, it would serve its purpose. It had to. They set aside two large, flat boards to use as paddles. All they needed was the injured mermaid to wake up.

Restlessness grew in Azure with every hour that ticked by. She knew her kind healed quicker than humans, so she was surprised at how much the leg injury affected her friend. The wound was deep. She couldn't deny that. But it shouldn't have caused Ocevia's lengthy unconsciousness. The wound was already mostly healed.

When they returned to the back room for a late lunch, Ocevia's turquoise eyes were bloodshot, but were finally opened. Rushing to her friend's side, Azure dropped to her knees beside her.

"What happened?" Ocevia's voice was rough from sleep, and Azure lifted the glass of water to her friend's lips. Ocevia tried to drink, but she sputtered in her eagerness to consume too much at once.

"I was going to ask you the same thing. You showed up with a giant gash on your leg and then passed out as we tried to stop the bleeding. You've been sleeping ever since." Ocevia rubbed her hand down her leg and winced when she grazed the bandages. Azure pushed her friend's hand away from the wound. "How did you get that injury?"

Ocevia blinked and then ran her hands along her face as though checking for more wounds. She seemed to be in a daze, likely from blood loss and too much sleep. "I don't really remember much after seeing the merbitches in the water." That was what Azure was afraid of. Her spine stiffened as she poured more water into her friend's mouth, slowly this time, so she wouldn't choke again. "I overheard them talking about finding you, so I followed them." Ocevia twisted the shell necklace around her throat and stared at the wall of dripping water. "I was beneath the sea when something pulled Oona in and then I was dragged into the depths during the chaos. Someone's dagger got me in the leg."

Azure wiped the water from Ocevia's chin. "Did they survive the attack? From the creature, I mean."

Ocevia shrugged and reached for the water again, taking a large gulp before leaning back on her elbows. Azure handed the glass to Elios so he could refill it. "I'm not sure if they made it. I drifted to the bottom after I got hurt. It took a while for me to make it back to the surface. I had to shift and swim as a human. My tail wouldn't function properly with the gash."

Elios handed the water back to Azure and added another log to the fire before sitting next to them. Ocevia glanced at him before returning her eyes to her friend. "And who is he?"

Azure shot her a sidelong glance before answering. "This is Elios. I pulled him off a rock outcropping after the shipwreck and brought him here."

Ocevia scanned Elios from head to toe, her stare almost clinical before she grinned at their near nakedness. "I see."

Azure huffed as she stood, knowing she could hide nothing from Ocevia. If anyone knew when she wasn't telling the truth, it was her best friend. Deciding it was better not to explain than to be caught lying, she dug through their fruit stores and handed Elios a mango. Using his dagger, he cut it into chunks for the injured mermaid.

After composing her face, Azure sat beside Ocevia again, handing her bite-sized pieces of the fruit. Many hours passed since they'd encountered her injured in the front of the cave, and she needed fuel to regain her strength. They needed her to improve in order to leave the island.

"Elios and I made a raft this morning. We can't stay here now that the others have found us. We need to leave as soon as possible."

"Good plan," Ocevia said around a bite of fruit. Juice dribbled from her mouth, making her look very much like a toddler at that moment. Azure tried to stifle a giggle but failed. "Any idea where you're headed?"

Azure glanced at Elios, who shrugged. "We haven't discussed it, but I think you mean 'we.' Looks like you're stuck with us for a while."

"I'll be fine." Ocevia said, waving her hand dismissively. She tried to stand, only to hiss and fall back to the ground. "On second thought, I guess I'll be a third-wheel for a while."

Elios chuckled, and Azure glared at him. He lifted his mango covered hands as his face fell into something more innocent. "What?"

Azure rolled her eyes. "Don't encourage this one." She pointed a finger at Ocevia. "She's trouble."

Her friend made a doe-like expression, mimicking Elios' own innocence, and Azure rolled her eyes again. With Elios and Ocevia as her travel companions, she would never get a moment's rest.

"So, when do we leave?" Ocevia was not strong enough to stand, but she held herself in a sitting position with little effort. Azure's shoulders were a little lighter at the sight.

"First light," said Elios, looking to Azure for confirmation. She nodded.

They would wait until first light, the time most mermaids slept, hoping those hunting them would be resting.

Azure wondered if Oona and Lucia ever made it back to Miris, or if there were new predators to run from—new enemies whose faces they did not yet know. Although she knew it was wrong, she hoped Oona and Lucia had not survived their encounter with the Kraken. They were intrinsically evil, and she reminded herself of that whenever guilt struck and reminded her that wishing death on someone was wrong. Even if administering death was her life's purpose, he couldn't stop those human emotions from reemerging at the worst times.

Oona and Lucia enjoyed killing, and if they'd survived the Kraken attack, they would return to Miris and then come back to kill all three of them. Neither Azure nor her two companions would be spared. So yes, Azure wished them to be dead, but the remnants of her humanity tormented her for the sentiment.

"Yes. Today, Elios and I will gather more food and pack up any supplies we need, so we're ready to leave in the morning."

Azure glanced around the cave, at the comfortable space they had made. Sure, it was no home, but it was the most luxury she'd experienced since being shackled to the ocean, and she

doubted they would find another cave with a hot spring in the future. She didn't even know how far they would have to travel before finding somewhere safe to stay. No place was out of Miris' reach. Wherever they settled next, safety would trump comfort.

"What about me?" Ocevia asked, a sticky orange strip of juice trailing down her forearm as she took another bite of mango. Azure laughed.

"Well, first, you need a bath." Ocevia's eyebrow arched as she continued. "Next, you'll rest. Elios and I will paddle the raft until you're well enough to help."

Ocevia scoffed. "I can help. And I don't really want to climb back into the sea to bathe right now, but thanks. I don't know if you realize, but my last trek in that water was not so great. Wet my tail? Yes. Submerge in the sea? No."

Snorting, Azure handed Ocevia the glass of water. "You lost a lot of blood, so no, you aren't paddling yet. Also, we have a hot spring here."

"And you're just telling me this now?" The injured mermaid scowled; her tone full of mock-offense.

"Sorry. I must have forgotten on account of you bleeding out and all. My mistake. It's over there." Azure gestured toward the pool before taking a bite of mango.

Ocevia's head swiveled toward the steaming hot spring, and her eyes sparkled at the sight. "You and your boyfriend have got to carry me over there. It's been so long since I've sat in a hot bath. There aren't many that we can go to."

Like a baby, Ocevia lifted her arms in a demand to be carried. Azure didn't have time to respond to her friend calling Elios her boyfriend before he scooped up the injured mermaid, silencing Ocevia. Lifting her with ease, he took her to the pool and set her down onto a stone ledge just inside the water.

Ocevia let out an over-exaggerated groan, but it was clear she enjoyed the spring as much as they did. She luxuriated in the water for a few moments before shifting into her mermaid form, teeth-clenched against the pain that made her complexion pale. Leaving her to wash up, Azure and Elios ventured out into the forest to gather supplies.

There were only a few hours left until the sun slumbered, and neither of them wanted to be out in the open when the mermaids began their nightly hunt. There was no guarantee that mermaids wouldn't be out during the day, especially since Oona and Lucia had attacked them before midday, but nightfall would increase the number of predators they encountered.

They needed to exercise caution when traveling by day, but Azure hoped that staying out of the water would help them avoid detection. If all else failed, they would have to rely on their small cache of handmade weapons to defend themselves. Neither served to settle the anxious fluttering in Azure's stomach, but there was nothing more they could do to prepare for their journey.

"I was thinking." Elios dropped a handful of berries in the handmade sack she held as he spoke. "If we can make it to the kingdom of Avrearyn, we could travel inland by horseback, or on foot, if we must, to Ceveasea. We can seek sanctuary there. I have a friend there who owes me a favor."

Azure's movements slowed as she pondered his words. Traveling inland would take them further from Miris' reach, but it could also put her and Ocevia in danger of losing their tails if they couldn't get to water in time. She didn't know if it was a risk they could afford to take.

Her chest tightened as more worries plagued her, and her lungs protested the lack of oxygen. "How far would the trek over land be?" If their trip was landlocked for too long, they would have to travel along the coast rather than inland, if possible. She would risk her own life, but she couldn't do the same with Ocevia's, or Elios'.

Elios' eyebrows drew together as he seemed to consider her question. "We can dock in the port city of Starspell. From there, the trip through the mountain pass should take less than a week." He scanned her face. "Are you worried about being too far from the sea?"

She shrugged. "I've never mentioned it before, but mermaids need to submerge in water at least once every twenty-four hours. If we don't, according to Miris, we'll rot from the waist down."

He grimaced and dropped the wood he held, wrapping his arms around her. "Don't worry. There are places along the way where we can stop. There are creeks, even a few hot springs. It won't be a problem. I will pour water over you with a bottle if I have to."

A familiar redness blossomed on the apples of Azure's cheeks as she stood on the tips of her toes and kissed him. The past twelve hours had been stressful and busy, but the dull ache between her thighs from the night before lingered, and his sweet words made her yearn to be alone with him again, to be in a place where they could let their guards down to just be together. "How could you make something like that sound so sexy?"

He grinned and pressed his lips to hers again, the kiss full of promise as she leaned into his warm body. Just being beside him made her feel safer. He was so solid, so strong. She drank in his intoxicating scent while his tongue caressed hers, leaving her breathless and filled with desire as he pulled away.

Picking up the pile of wood he neglected, Elios tipped his head in the cave's direction. "We should head back. It'll be dark soon."

Azure didn't look forward to returning to the damp darkness after enjoying the sun's rays and nature's fresh scent, but the cave offered them safety. Well, as much safety as they could get while surrounded by Miris' territory.

In that realization, her decision was made. The only way they could ensure their relative safety was to travel as far away from the sea as possible. They would do as Elios suggested, take their raft to Avrearyn and then travel by land to Ceveasea. As long as there was enough water for her and Ocevia to wet their tails, maybe they could finally sleep with both eyes closed.

Chapter Eleven
Leaving the Island

The atmosphere in the cave was heavy that night, or at least it was for Azure. The upcoming trip weighed on her. There was so much more at stake than her own safety. Ocevia was injured, and Elios was human. None of them were invincible, but Elios was more fragile than she and her best friend were. Even though he was trained with weapons, he bled like any other mortal man, and he didn't have the healing abilities that she and Ocevia had. That alone was enough to keep her up that night.

Mermaids were not eternal, but they lived far longer than humans. Once turned, aging slowed to a glacial pace, extending their lifespans to five times that of a human. Aside from extended lifespans, a mermaid's expedient healing made them harder to kill. Sure, severe injuries could ground them for a day or two, but they could survive wounds that the average human could not. That, and Elios binding her wound, was what prevented Ocevia from dying from the wound to her thigh.

The anticipation was too great for Azure to close her eyes and rest, so she got very little sleep. Waiting until she saw the sky begin to lighten through the corridor, she woke Ocevia and Elios. She had already bagged up their food and supplies, even fashioning a makeshift sail small enough to hang from branches on their raft, before her companions ever stirred. The sail would likely fall over but paddling for countless miles would be painful and exhausting. Anything that could give them a break was worth a shot.

"How are you feeling, Ocevia? Any pain?" Azure folded their leather blankets while her friend pulled on the primitive shoes made from salvaged materials. The blond was visibly flustered by the flimsy material. "We'll have to find a way to get us proper shoes before we start our hike into the mountains."

Elios passed behind them, stopping to give Azure a kiss, before carrying their packs into the front chamber of the cave. "I have credits in Avrearyn and Ceveasea. You can get whatever you want."

Ocevia's eyebrows shot up as he left the room. Azure shook her head, knowing what her friend was thinking.

"No. We are not going on a shopping spree with his coin."

She stuck her tongue out at her friend before following behind her lover, sack of blankets in hand. "I think this is the last of it. I'll help you bring the raft to the beach."

Elios tugged on the straps that sealed their bags, checking that they were secure. "We should wait until we're ready to bring Ocevia down. I don't want to chance it floating away. We can bring it closer, though, if you want to take that side."

Azure followed his direction, hefting up her half of the raft. She cleared the opening of all its branches and stones in the middle of the night, so they exited with ease. If not for the raft being in two pieces, it certainly would not have made it out, but thankfully, they'd had the forethought to keep the structure separate until they passed through the exit.

Once outside, they strapped the two sides together and placed the sail into slots Azure had carved to secure it. If it didn't hold, they would have had to do a lot of paddling.

It was a relief to see the wind was on their side as they made their way to the coastline. If it continued to blow north, they wouldn't need the paddles. However, chances were that the wind would eventually shift.

Azure stared out over the horizon for a moment while Elios tested the bindings that connected the two halves. She couldn't help but wonder if any mermaids lurked in the shadowy depths, preparing to pull them under. When she crouched to help him, he winked and swatted her hand away. She grinned, moving to check the sail. It seemed solid, and at least, for the moment, it stood.

Transporting Ocevia to the raft was the biggest chore. The stubborn mermaid fought to walk on her own the entire way, even though she had struggled, and failed, to put much weight on her injured leg. The argument was settled after she took the first few steps and Elios threw her over his shoulder, carrying her down the sloping terrain. She complained—loudly—but eventually gave up the fight they all knew she wouldn't win.

It was bittersweet to leave the place that had served as their temporary home for so many days. Although it wasn't as safe as they'd hoped, it was more comfortable than any of the caves Azure frequented over the past three years. She was, however, excited to see new places, and to be traveling further from Miris' grasp, if they could manage to get out of the sea alive.

"You know." Ocevia grumbled as Elios set her down in the raft. "I'm never going to strengthen my leg if you don't let me try."

Narrowing his eyes at her, he pushed the raft into the water. "You can practice when we're in Avrearyn. We need to get out of here while it's still early."

Azure smirked as her friend crossed her arms across her chest and pouted. Once the raft floated in the shallows, Elios held it steady as Azure climbed inside, grabbing her paddle. She sat near the front of the craft and stuck the long paddle into the sea, holding it as still as she could while Elios climbed into his seat at the back, paddle in hand. He used the wood to push off from the shore, and they were off.

As the sun continued its ascent, Azure regretted not preparing a canopy. By midafternoon, the scorching rays beat down without remorse, baking them. After the first couple of hours, the wind quieted, making the water still, and the sail obsolete. She was glad they weren't paddling against the current, but she hoped the wind would blow in their direction again before her arms gave out. Her limbs always got plenty of exercise from swimming, but the repetitive motion was still tiresome after a while.

The trio remained quiet as they traversed the silent waters, knowing the sound would travel. They didn't want to draw any attention to themselves.

Having no task on the raft, Ocevia covered her face with a cloth and fell asleep. It was for the best. The blond mermaid wasn't exactly known for being the quiet type, at least not around Azure.

The sky turned overcast a little after midday and, to Azure's relief, the wind began to blow in their direction again. Once the sail roughly began to do its job, she carefully set down her paddle on the floor of the raft and dug into a bag, sectioning off food for them to snack on while they rested their arms.

"If this wind keeps up, we may reach the coast by tomorrow." Elios stared at the horizon, as though he could already see the city of Starspell in the distance. Azure hoped they would arrive by the next day, because being stuck on a raft in open water was the worst place for them to be. It wasn't safe.

Azure had only ever been to her homeland, Thatia, and the sea. She didn't know what to expect from the cities of Starspell and Ceveasea. And since she was forbidden, she hadn't been to Thatia since Miris cursed her. Since then, her only experience with a city was glimpsing its lights in the distance while patrolling the shipping channels for souls to claim. It wasn't a life that offered variety, but she guessed being cursed never did. It was meant to be a punishment, and it was.

"Have you ever been there?"

Elios took a bite of his fish and nodded. "I've been to every kingdom that surrounds the Lamalis Sea, and some lands beyond the coast. I haven't been to Starspell in about five months, but I have plenty of contacts and credits there. We won't have a problem getting what we need once we get there."

A lightness filled her chest at the thought of not struggling, being able to live on land again with adequate food and shelter. She never thought she'd return to the human lands. Even if she couldn't seek her sister, it would still be exciting to be among humans once again. To see humans, and not be forced to take their lives, was a thrilling prospect.

"So, do you know where we'll stay when we get there? Before we head into the mountains, I mean."

Elios tossed the pit of his fruit into the water, and the tiny fish immediately swam to the surface and started pecking at it. "There's a tavern I frequent when I'm in port. We can rent a couple of rooms there for the night. But we shouldn't hang around the city for long before moving inland."

Azure leaned over the side of the raft to watch the fish. "I agree. Miris will send people to the coast once they can't find us on any of the islands. If they aren't already there now." The thought made her stomach turn.

Elios nodded and grabbed his paddle, beginning to help move the raft along. Azure did the same. The sooner they were off the water, the better.

Before the sun set, Azure and Ocevia were forced to enter the water to prevent their tails from rotting. Azure didn't feel comfortable getting back into the sea, but it was necessary. Getting off and back on the raft was a balancing act, and they nearly flipped the entire craft over upon reentry. Thankfully, that didn't happen.

After making back onto the raft with no major incident, they began rowing with renewed vigor. Putting distance between the point they entered the water, and themselves, was imperative, and she hoped they were long gone by the time their scents made it back to Miris, or her people. If they were surrounded by the water, there would be no hope of escape, especially for Elios.

As the long hours passed, strong winds billowed their sail until nightfall, threatening a storm that never came. Elios and Azure napped in shifts, enjoying the paddling reprieve. One person always remained awake to keep an eye out for danger and to ensure the boat stayed on course. When night crept up on them, the wind died down again, and they returned to paddling.

Ocevia woke for a bit in the evening to eat but fell quickly back to sleep. Her excessive exhaustion worried Azure, but there wasn't anything she could do to help other than hope her friend continued to improve.

Progress slowed dramatically once the sun slept. They did their best not to upset the water, because, unlike during the day, mermaids were out hunting for souls beneath the moon, and they didn't want to be among the damned. There were no shipping channels nearby, which was their only saving grace. They had spotted no ships since they'd boarded their handmade vessel, but that didn't mean mermaids weren't around. Small talk was not worth the risk of being caught, so they drifted in silence, only paddling if their course was altered.

The trip was relatively uneventful, making it difficult for Azure to keep her eyes open. Dark shapes passed beneath them occasionally, but she was confident the shapes were nothing more than large fish. She thought about the Kraken occasionally, but the creature did not make another appearance.

The desire to ask Ocevia more about what she saw that day was strong, but she didn't dare try to hold a conversation while on the silent sea. Plus, in order to get an answer, Ocevia needed to remain awake, which seemed impossible for the injured mermaid. Whether Ocevia was suffering from exhaustion or boredom, Azure didn't know. Either way, her friend seemed to think that, since she couldn't help paddle or navigate, she should remain unconscious until they reached the shore.

When the rough outline of land appeared on the horizon in midafternoon on the following day, excitement spread throughout the raft. Azure looked over her shoulder at Elios, and her heart skipped a beat at the brilliant grin that graced his lips, his blue eyes bright in the sun. "We're almost there, ladies."

Ocevia watched the land with childlike wonder, as though she'd never seen something so incredible. "I haven't been to the human lands in a very long time. Not since I was a child. I don't remember what it was like."

Pain tinged in Azure's heart at her friend's words. She couldn't imagine being trapped in servitude since childhood. Being taken after barely becoming an adult was hard enough. At least Azure had plenty of memories of growing up in the human lands, a luxury her friend didn't have. Memories of her parents before they died. Memories of spending time with her family. Memories of her sister, and the one of losing Daneliya that day on the beach. The ache in Azure's chest deepened as she wondered if it was better to not remember at all. She didn't know the story of Ocevia's past, only that she was cursed as a child, but the blond always made it very clear that she recalled little, and didn't want to speak of her family, so it remained a mystery.

Taking a cursory glance around, Azure confirmed they were alone on the water and shifted into her mermaid form. "We should wet our tails before we reach land. Who knows how long it will be before we can do it again?" Remaining seated, she filled two glass bottles, handing one to her friend before pouring some of it over her dry tail. "I don't want to attempt getting in the water again. It'll draw attention if we flip the raft so close to the shore, not to mention spreading our scents. We'll have to do our best by wetting them from here."

Ocevia nodded and shifted into her own mermaid form, making the vessel even more crowded. The iridescence of their tails reflected the sun's rays beautifully, casting a sparkling kaleidoscope of colors around them. Elios continued to paddle, but his eyes were wide as he watched them. It wasn't his first time seeing their true forms, but he still seemed fascinated with them. Azure flushed under his stare as she used her hand to spread the water across the dry patches on her purple tail. She consciously slowed her motions, watching Elios' reaction, and she wasn't disappointed as his eyes traced every sweeping pass she made. The corner of his mouth twitched with a repressed smirk as realization spread across his face. He knew exactly what she was doing.

"Just for the record," Ocevia interrupted. "I am not sharing a room with you two lovebirds."

Elios laughed, but Azure buried her face in her hands, mortification deepening the color on her cheeks. It was exactly what she got for trying to be sexy.

After Ocevia's comment, Azure ended her attempt at a seductive show, at least while her friend was watching. Ensuring that the last of her tail was moistened, she shifted back into her human form, grabbing her paddle as they moved steadily closer to the coastal city of Starspell.

From what Azure could tell, as they neared Starspell harbor just after sunset, the city was bustling. Stars sparkled under the darkening sky, the mountainous backdrop framing the city. Candlelight illuminated nearly every window. Ocevia's face shone with marvel as she tried to absorb all the sights. Azure understood exactly how her friend felt because the same excitement buzzed through her veins as well.

"My friend's tavern is close to the harbor." Elios' voice seemed to echo out over the calm sea. "So, once we dock this contraption and gather our things, we'll go straight there. He can arrange for clothing to be brought to the tavern for us, and we can order food and drinks. It'll be comfortable there."

The crushing weight on Azure's shoulders eased with every swipe of the paddle. As they drew closer, sounds of the city reached their ears. Upbeat music came from somewhere along the strip of buildings that appeared to be the main street, bringing a smile to her face. With the color of the sky deepening by the minute, she couldn't make out the fine details as they approached, but her pulse raced in anticipation. She couldn't wait to see Starspell in all its glory when the sun returned.

Chapter Twelve
STARSPELL

T he tavern was, as Elios promised, close to the harbor. Once they'd moored their raft, secretly hoping to never see it again, the trio gathered their belongings, and Elios carried a surly Ocevia as they made their way to the main strip of buildings.

From the outside, the tavern looked intimate and cheerful. Sandstone bricks and marble detailing made up the building's outer structure. It was impossible to see through the sand-beaten windows, but the sounds of cutlery and drinking glasses traveled outside. Tingling excitement raced through Azure's body as she opened the metal door and held it for Elios to pass through as he held the grumpy blond. They were instantly greeted by laughing voices and the smell of home-cooked food.

The tavern was packed, which made Azure think they must have delicious food and drinks to draw in such a full house. Several long tables were occupied by a variety of patrons, conversation filling the space. Even the stools at the bar were occupied. The bartender, who Elios nodded at from across the room, was engaged in his own discussion with an elderly man who wore an eye patch but approached them before they managed to make it through the crowd.

Silver, well-groomed hair framed a long, cheerful face. The tall, slender man looked like he was in his middle years, forty or fifty, and Azure could tell how much he loved working in the tavern by the gleam in his hazel eyes.

"Elios," the silver-haired man said as he patted Elios on the shoulder so hard, he nearly dropped Ocevia, who was still grumbling to be put down. Obliging the mermaid, he chuckled and set her down on shaky legs. Slipping behind him, Ocevia took up the spot next to Azure, leaning on her friend for support, although it didn't appear like she needed it. After a few days of rest, she seemed to have regained most of her leg strength. Azure was relieved to see her friend's improvement after worrying over how much she'd been sleeping.

Elios reached out and shook the man's hand; his face lit up with a genuine smile. "Vasso. Good to see you, Old Friend. Business looks like it's going well."

Vasso's smile broadened as he wrapped his arm around Elios' shoulders and scanned the room full of chatting people. The band, made up of three men playing a fiddle, a horn, and a drum, entertained the crowd with upbeat music. "Business has been great." He turned back to Elios and arched an eyebrow. "What brings you back to Starspell?"

Azure shifted from foot to foot anxiously. They hadn't discussed a cover story. Elios looked back at her and flashed a reassuring smile. "We're just passing through. Probably won't stay more than the night."

Vasso seemed to pick up on a hidden meaning and nodded. "Off the record it is. One room or two?"

"Two, but near each other, if possible. We need supplies as well. My companions will need clothes, and we need something to eat. We have, unfortunately, had to travel with not much more than the clothes on our backs." Azure wrapped her arms around her chest, suddenly painfully aware that her leather clothing was not much more than undergarments. She was glad for the tavern's dim ambiance.

"Are my credits still adequate?"

Vasso smiled and patted Elios on the shoulder again. "Your credits are plenty. Let me grab those keys for you, and you can get these ladies settled upstairs. I'll have food and beverages brought up while Chryssa rustles up some clothes for them. The stores are closed at this hour, but she should be able to scrounge up a few things until morning."

Elios reached for Azure's hand, intertwining their fingers as the middle-aged man walked away. The pass of his thumb on her palm soothed her racing heart. Her anxiety had reached new highs as she stood in the busy tavern underdressed, dirty, and not-quite human. It was unlikely the patrons realized what she and Ocevia were, but she knew they didn't belong there, and that was enough to make her unease grow.

Vasso returned with two keys, and Elios took them, leading the way up an obscure stairwell nestled in the back of the tavern. He'd had to help Ocevia climb the stairs, but only for support. She was insistent to do it all by herself. Thankfully, most of the patrons were too deep into their revelry and did not give them a second glance as the shirtless man and two scantily dressed women, one with a heavy limp, made their way across the room and out of sight. Azure cringed at the thoughts they would have formed if they had noticed them.

A few sconces along the stairs and hallway lit the path, and the dull illumination made it difficult to observe their surroundings. Elios was quite familiar with the place, however, and had no problem finding their rooms.

Unlocking the last door on the right, he motioned to Ocevia. "Make yourself comfortable. One of us will come to knock when Vasso sends up food and clothing. Get some rest. There are usually towels in the bathing room, and there is a bathtub for your tail."

Ocevia needed no more convincing. The moment she heard there was a bathtub, she darted into the candlelit guest room and slammed the door behind her. Azure snickered as she waited for Elios to point out their own room. Her stomach was aflutter at the thought of spending the night with him, in an actual room, in a proper bed.

The human lands were forbidden, but she had broken so many rules since rescuing Elios that it no longer mattered. Screwed either way, Azure decided to just enjoy herself. She hadn't spent the night in a human dwelling, felt the comfort of a mattress or blankets in over three years, and she intended to relish every second of it. With her new romance blooming, there was much more to look forward to than just the comfort of a bed. She would finally be able to feel Elios' skin against hers again. Her body heated at the thought.

Azure and Elios' room was the last room on the left, directly across the hall from Ocevia's. She wondered if Elios always took the room farthest away from the tavern, and why Vasso was so familiar with Elios needing transactions "off the record." She knew little about Elios, other than him traveling the world and staying away from his family. There was so much more she wanted to know about him, but she put those questions on hold, at least for the night.

Elios unlocked the door, allowing Azure to enter the room. It was small, but cozy. A large wooden bedframe took up most of the space, but there was also a small table with two chairs and an armoire in the main bedroom area. A door opened into a small bathing room with a sink, toilet, and soaking tub. A sliver of moonlight filtered in through a window that looked out over the sea. Elios lit several candles around the suite, creating a romantic glow. The room smelled of dust, but Azure opened the window, letting the sea breeze in to cool the room and freshen the scent. She breathed in deeply, the fragrance she knew so well bringing about mixed emotions.

Elios continued doing tasks around the room as Azure gazed out at the star-filled sky's reflection on the calm surface of the water. "I've never seen the sea like this."

Elios stopped what he was doing and wrapped his arms around her waist, peering over her shoulder to take in the view. "Like what?" He placed a kiss on the curve of her neck, sending shivers through her body.

"Sparkling. It's beautiful."

A knock on the door interrupted their moment. A barmaid, carrying a steaming tray of food and wine, entered the room, dropping off their meal and leaving without a word. Azure's mouth watered at the delicious aroma that filled the room. They had eaten so little over the past week, and neither the fruit nor the dried fish had given off such an appealing scent.

The hearty stew and buttered bread made her stomach growl, but Azure eyed the wine decanter warily. She was thirsty, but had never tried an alcoholic beverage before, so she was unsure how it would affect her. Still, she didn't plan to turn it away.

"Are you hungry?" Elios asked as he poured three glasses of wine. She nodded enthusiastically.

"I'll get Ocevia. I'm sure she's ready to eat as well." Elios began removing the bowls from the tray and setting the table as she headed across the hall.

She knocked on Ocevia's door, but no one answered. After a few silent moments, Azure grew concerned and nudged the still unlocked door open to peek inside. Singing greeted her immediately, pushing the worst-case scenarios that had begun to form from her mind.

"Ocevia?" She called as she slipped into the room. "Food is ready."

The singing stopped, and the sound of water splashing followed. "Hey! I'm in the tub."

Smiling, she joined her friend in the bathing room. Ocevia filled in the bath, the end of her tail hanging over the edge. The floor around the tub was drenched. Azure chuckled. "You're lucky it's only me and not one of the wait staff checking in on you."

Her friend flourished her hand as she lifted a glass to rinse her golden hair. "Well, they shouldn't enter my room uninvited."

Rolling her eyes, Azure nodded toward the bedroom door. "It was unlocked."

Ocevia grimaced. "I haven't been in the human lands since I was a child. I couldn't figure out how to lock it. I don't know how to use half the stuff in here. It took me forever just to figure out how to turn the water on."

Realization washed over Azure like icy rain, and guilt burned closely behind. She'd left Ocevia to her own devices when her friend knew nothing of her surroundings. "I'm sorry, Ocevia. I should have shown you around and explained things to you."

With a smirk, Ocevia pulled the plug from the drain and shifted her tail back into long legs. "Don't worry about it. I'm the one who ran off at the promise of a tub. If you and your hunk of manliness give me food and clothes, I'm sure I can figure out how to use the bed on my own. I don't plan on doing much other than sleeping after I eat."

Azure headed for the exit while Ocevia dried off with a fluffy white towel. "I'll bring in a plate of food and a glass of wine for you while you dry off. I expect they'll bring up clothing soon. I'll be right back."

Elios was already in the open doorway of their room, holding a bowl of steaming stew with a piece of bread and a glass of wine, when she walked into the hallway.

"Chryssa should be here with clothes soon. It'll be enough to get you and Ocevia through the night at least. How is she?"

The scent of the rich stew wafted by Azure's nose, making her stomach rumble again. She was hungrier than she'd realized. "She's doing well, but I feel bad for not realizing she wouldn't know how to work anything. It's been too long since she's been in a human structure. She managed to figure out how to run a bath on her own, though, so she's quite content."

Azure reopened Ocevia's door, food in hand. Her friend kneeled across the room, stark naked, trying to light the fireplace. Quickly kicking the door shut behind herself, Azure set the dishes down on the table and grabbed the fire starter from the mantle. Crouching beside her friend, she showed her how to light the fire.

One of the first things Ocevia had taught her when she was first cursed was how to build a fire out in nature, but they never had the convenience of a fire starter in the caves. Azure was reminded of how ill-prepared her friend was for the human world. There was so much she needed to be taught.

Ocevia paid close attention as Azure went through a few tries before the fire roared to life. Clearly, her friend wasn't the only one who needed practice with using human items. Elios knocked as they worked on the fire and cracked the door open, reaching his hand in, a few pieces of clothing hanging from his fingers.

Azure passed the clothes to Ocevia, quickly showing her how to put the nightdress on. Human clothes were one more thing her friend had no experience with. Mermaids didn't wear such things. Before returning to her room, she showed her friend how to use some of the room's basic amenities, including how to use the toilet.

Dinner was lukewarm by the time Azure returned to their room, but it didn't matter. She would have happily devoured the stew, even if it were cold. She was that famished. Ever the gentleman, Elios sat at the table, waiting for her to join him before he ate. He stood as she approached, pushing in her chair once she sat, before returning to his own. Azure couldn't help but blush at his consideration.

"Is she all settled now?"

She nodded and took a sip of the red wine, grimacing at the taste. It was sweet at first, but the aftertaste was quite bitter. Still, she took another sip. "I don't think she likes human clothing much, but she's enjoying the food, and I'm pretty certain she's going to jump on the bed even though I told her not to."

Elios chuckled and refilled his glass from the decanter. "After all of her time away, I think she deserves to jump on the bed." Azure completely agreed, but she couldn't help worrying about the injury that somehow still exhausted her friend.

Chapter Thirteen
The Good Parts

After being taunted by the rich stew's aroma for what felt like hours, Azure finally ate. Even at room temperature, it was still better than anything she'd tasted over the last three years. She ate enthusiastically, realizing after she'd almost licked her bowl that Elios was staring at her, and it was most likely not because she looked sexy. She probably looked more like a rabid animal than an alluring woman. Inwardly, she cringed, but it didn't stop her from licking the butter off her fingers.

Setting the dish down gingerly, she downed the rest of her wine to hide the awkwardness she felt, trying her best not to grimace at the bitter taste. "Would you like more stew? I can have more brought up." Elios' face was neutral, but she didn't doubt was holding back a laugh at her voracious eating.

Azure hiccupped before she could answer, and she realized she'd consumed the wine a little too quickly. Her head felt lighter, as though it was floating, but she guessed that was the point of drinking the bitter liquid. The sensation made her giddy, and she covered her mouth as she giggled, making Elios smile mischievously. "I think I've had enough food, but I would like more wine."

Elios arched a questioning eyebrow, and it seemed he didn't think she needed another glass, but he still poured her a small one. She didn't complain about the half-filled glass. It was probably for the best. She didn't want to drown in the bathtub.

"Are you ready to get cleaned up? It's been a long couple of days. I'm sure you're as tired as I am."

The bathing room seemed so much farther away than it did before they'd had dinner. Azure gazed at it with longing, willing her legs to carry her. It was best to submerge her tail whenever she was given the chance, but the way the world spun beneath her made the trek across the room seem perilous.

She gave a slow nod, trying not to make the floor tilt more than it already did. Chuckling, Elios stood, offering her his arm. Half supporting, and half carrying her, he guided her to the bathing room.

Azure sat on a stool beside the tub while her lover filled it with steaming water, watching him with a lust-filled gaze. After the water was shut off, he helped her to remove her handmade clothes. The bar owner provided a simple tunic and a set of trousers for both women, and she looked forward to wearing them. To wear real clothing, after so long, was an exciting prospect, but first she needed to wash away the days of grime and saltwater that clung to her skin. Holding onto Elios for balance, she climbed into the warm water and shifted her legs to her tail.

After all their nights bathing together in the hot spring pool, it was strange to be in the bath alone, but she barely fit by herself, especially in her mermaid form. Elios offered to leave the room and give her privacy, but she asked him to stay. They hadn't spent much time apart since she pulled him from the sea that fateful night, and she didn't want to start now. Sitting on the stool beside her, he kept her company while she soaked her tail.

They chatted while he used a cup to pour warm water over her. It was such a simple act, but it felt incredibly sensual as she leaned back and let him take over washing her hair. With her eyes closed, every sensation was magnified. The scent of the lavender shampoo, mixed with traces of sweat from Elios' body, and the feel of his powerful hands massaging her scalp, all worked to intensify the desire building inside her.

It had been days since he'd taken her for the first time, and she craved that feeling again. She wanted the fingers that were running along her scalp to travel lower, to caress her body until they sent her over the edge once more. She kept those thoughts to herself, deciding to wait until they were in bed to act on them. She wanted to know what it would be like to enjoy each other on a mattress instead of a wet stone floor, but they had all night.

When it came time for Elios to bathe, Azure stayed with him. After everything they went through together, it felt unnatural to be apart. The initial buzz from the wine wore off as she had bathed, leaving a warm, carefree feeling in its wake. She stared, shameless, at Elios' perfect body as droplets of water slid down the curve of his muscled chest and merged with the pool of water at his waist. He didn't seem to mind her attention. If anything, he enjoyed it. Every time she met his eye, he was grinning at her, his blue eyes bright in the candlelight. When he washed the hardness below his waist, he gave it an extra caress for her.

"See something you like, Azure?"

The flush returned to her face, but she didn't deny it. "Why don't you get out of the tub? I'll show you exactly what parts of you I like."

The second the sultry words left her mouth, Azure was shocked at herself, and from the look on Elios' face, they had surprised him as well. The look of surprise quickly faded, morphing into a heated stare. He finished washing in record time, drying off just as quickly.

Throwing his towel to the side, he wrapped his muscular arms around her, carrying her to the bed.

"I hope you didn't plan on getting much sleep tonight, Azure."

His deep voice sent a thrill of anticipation through her, and she bit his bottom lip playfully.

"Who needs sleep?"

CHAPTER FOURTEEN
SECRETS

*W*aves crashed against the shore as the briny scent of the sea flooded Azure's nose. She looked around frantically, taking in the scene, forcing herself to process what was happening. Her heart raced, fear coursing through her veins, but she didn't know why she was experiencing such terror. She didn't see any reason to be afraid, even with the violence of the surf.

She knew this beach so well. It was the same beach she'd played on as a child. Dark clouds loomed in the distance, the ominous sign of a storm brewing. A giggle rang out across the deserted sand, a sound of happiness, and she whipped around to look for the source.

Seven-year-old Daneliya played along the beach, jumping and splashing in the water. Azure smiled at her sister's joy. The little girl's laugh was infectious, but the happy expression died on her lips as a heavy sense of foreboding crushed her lungs. The scene was too familiar, and suddenly, her thundering pulse made sense.

"Daneliya, no!"

Arms outstretched to grab her little sister, Azure darted for the water, but she was too slow. The current caught the child, yanking her feet out from under her, and she disappeared beneath the surface. Diving into the water, Azure opened her eyes, desperately searching for Daneliya, but she wasn't there. Her sister was gone.

An incessant knocking woke Azure the following morning, and an empty stomach pulled her out of bed. Her head throbbed in time with each bang against their door, and she was thankful when Elios pulled on his trousers and answered. She fumbled with the ties of her borrowed tunic, seriously regretting all the wine she'd consumed the night before.

Her eyes widened when Elios opened the door, and she spotted Ocevia. Her best friend's blond hair was disheveled, and her tunic was only partially closed, exposing most of her chest. Dashing across the room, she grabbed Ocevia by the arm, pulling her inside.

"Ocevia," Azure worked to close her friend's tunic to cover her full breasts. "You can't stand in the hallway half-dressed."

Ocevia looked at her clothes with an incredulous glance. "I usually wear way less than this, Azure. You're being ridiculous."

Stifling a sigh, she placed her hands on Ocevia's shoulders. "Mermaids wear less, but humans don't. Remember, you're pretending to be human right now."

Ocevia didn't argue, and Azure exhaled in relief. "So, what's the plan for today?" The blond scrutinized them, like she was trying to decipher their body language, and Azure hoped their appearances didn't make last night's activities obvious. Not that her friend didn't already know they were lovers.

Elios sat at the foot of the bed and pulled on his boots, lacing them quickly. "Let's head down to the tavern for breakfast first." He glanced up at Azure, and she flushed under his gaze.

Their first night in a real bed was memorable, to say the least. She could still feel the absence of him inside her. "Or I can have it brought up, if you'd prefer." Ocevia's sprint toward the door was as obvious an answer as any.

Even at breakfast, the tavern was lively, filled with cheerful people, enjoying their food and chatting with each other. The trio grabbed a table in the corner and ordered three daily specials of eggs and fried potatoes. It wasn't the healthiest breakfast, but it was readily available. Plus, it was way better than dried fish.

Watching Ocevia dig into the greasy breakfast was worth the stomachache Azure knew she'd have later. They only ate what they could find in the sea and on the uninhabited islands they frequented. By the enthusiastic way the blond mermaid consumed her breakfast, moaning and groaning, it was clear she didn't remember food from the human lands but was enjoying it. With being taken at such a young age, it wasn't surprising.

To Azure's relief, a middle-aged woman, the bar owner's wife, according to Elios, dropped off several bags of clothing and supplies at their table as they were finishing their meal. The long tunics they wore were comfortable, but one outfit would not be enough for the long journey ahead. They collected the bags and headed for the stairs when Vasso approached them. Grabbing Elios by the wrist, he pulled him into a darkened hallway. Azure and Ocevia followed, a nervous pit forming in Azure's stomach.

They waited silently for Vasso to explain what was going on. His shifty eyes and secretive behavior were a stark contrast to his demeanor the night before. It frightened her, bringing the worst scenarios into her mind. Harder lines accented Elios' face as he frowned at the man, concern evident in his expression. Vasso looked around once more before he leaned in, his voice hardly more than a whisper.

"I don't mean to rush you off, Elios, but there were some individuals digging around in town late last night, looking for a woman with her description." He dipped his chin toward Azure, sending her stomach plummeting. "They came into the tavern after the three of you went to bed. I didn't recognize either of them under their heavy cloaks, but I ran their asses off. I doubt they've left the city, though. It's not safe for you here."

Elios rubbed his brows, looking frustrated, but not at all surprised. He seemed to expect this, but Azure was shocked at how quickly Miris' people had found them. Claustrophobia threatened to take hold of her at the threat of them being so close. "Send word to our contacts. We'll set out for Ceveasea today."

Vasso nodded and glanced at Azure and Ocevia before returning his worried gaze to Elios. "I can spare a few men from The Circle. I don't want you leaving with these ladies without a few extra swords."

Elios seemed to expect this as well. He nodded once before grabbing Azure's hand and leading them upstairs. She didn't know what The Circle was, but it was clear that Elios was more than just a drifter, more than just an adventurer. Whatever he was, he seemed to be important, and his dealings seemed to be dangerous. She tried to ignore the feeling of betrayal that began to take root, reminding herself that they hadn't known each other for very long. The story he'd told her was clearly not the entire truth, but he hadn't explicitly lied to her. Still, she was determined to learn everything in time.

Not speaking in the hallway, Elios led Azure and Ocevia into their room. "Take a moment to wet your tails while you can. I'll get our packs together. I know you understood what Vasso said. They're already here looking for us. If we don't get out of the city now, we may never be able to leave."

The pit in Azure's stomach twisted into a knot, tightening until it became hard to breathe. "Elios," she hesitated. "What is The Circle?"

His lips pressed together in a fine line, and he glanced around the room before taking her hands in his. "I promise to tell you everything once we're safe. But for now, we need to get moving. I'd imagine Vasso is preparing the horses and men now. The sooner we leave, the better. The longer we wait, the more danger you'll be in, we'll all be in."

It wasn't the answer Azure wanted, but he was right. With Miris' people already searching the city for them, time was of the essence. So, although she had so many questions, she grabbed two fresh pairs of trousers and boots out of the bag, handed a set to Ocevia, and rushed to the bathroom for a quick soak. The soft click of the guestroom door told her Ocevia had left to do the same.

By the time they returned downstairs with their belongings stuffed into a few satchels, Vasso had four horses and a few men, ready and waiting, in the alley behind the building. Vasso's wife, Chryssa, handed Elios a bag of filled water-skins and food, as well as another with what looked like bedding, before hugging him.

Everything felt too rushed, like they would never be able to stop running. All Azure wanted was to be able to stay in one place for a while, to breathe easily, and maybe even get some proper sleep. But, at least for now, that was still not an option. Instead, they approached their traveling party in the quiet alley, preparing to flee once again.

One of the men introduced himself as Dimitris Teresides. With vibrant red hair and a strong, masculine face, he appeared close to Elios' age, but his equally crimson beard made him look slightly older. His smile was warm as he greeted them, wrapping his arm around Elios' shoulder like they knew each other well. They chatted for a moment while the horses were saddled, and their belongings were stored in the saddlebags.

Ocevia's brow wrinkled as she shifted from foot to foot, eyeing the horses and men nervously while they waited. Moving closer, Azure grabbed her hand. "Are you okay?"

The blonde didn't take her eyes off the party preparing for their trek into the mountains. "I don't know how to ride a horse, Azure. That thing may kill me."

Azure barely managed to stifle a snicker. "I haven't ridden a horse since I was younger, and have barely any experience either, but I'm sure you won't be by yourself. You'll ride with one of those fine men." She flourished her hand toward the group, at the three suitable men who could take Ocevia on their journey atop his horse. All of them looked capable of watching over her.

Dimitris still talked with Elios as the men checked the saddles. The two other men who would travel with them were introduced as Markos and Aris.

Aris was older than Elios, probably in his early forties, but he was extremely attractive. All the men were. His long, golden hair was tied in a low ponytail, and would have probably reached his waist if not pulled back. His honey brown eyes were warm, although he'd said little more than his name since they'd met. Taller than the other three men, Aris' body looked built for battle, the tattoos on his arms telling of his adventures. He hadn't said much, but Azure knew he had many stories to share. She only hoped to hear them while on their journey.

Markos also appeared to be Elios' age, in his mid-twenties. He had similar boyish good looks to Elios, but his hair was black and shaggy, hanging to just above his shoulders, and his eyes were the color of spring grass. Both men also knew Elios, but everyone seemed to have a job to do. They must have been told the situation would be risky, as they kept small talk to a minimum. Well, except for Dimitris, who seemed to have a lot to say.

Ocevia watched the men with a thoughtful expression as the party said goodbye to Vasso, making Azure wonder what caused the sudden shift. With Ocevia, she could never tell.

"I want that one, I think." Ocevia spoke with so much conviction as she pointed at Markos, who stood near a horse that was the same color as his inky hair, chewing on a piece of straw. He, out of all the men, seemed the most uninterested in the women, but he had apparently caught her friend's eye.

Azure laughed and patted Ocevia on the back. "I'm not sure if you get to choose, but I'll see what I can do."

Azure approached Elios as he turned to her, holding out his hand to help her mount the horse. She glanced back at Ocevia, who wrung her hands nervously. Her usually chatty friend was silent, shy even. "I think she wants to ride with Markos."

Elios chuckled and winked at her before turning to the man still standing quietly beside his horse. "Hey, Markos," Elios called out. The man jerked at the sound of his name, clearly startled, before jogging over to them. Elios pointed at the blond female still standing near the back of the tavern. "Can you look after Ocevia for us?" Nodding, Markos headed over to Ocevia without a word.

Elios helped Azure into the saddle of their horse, Night Step, while Ocevia followed Markos to his own mount, Ocevia's expression almost bashful. The poor guy didn't know what he was getting into with Ocevia, but Azure hoped he would be a gentleman to her friend. While Azure knew little about the opposite sex, Ocevia knew even less.

Vasso and Chryssa waved goodbye as the group set off along the back alleys and toward the mountain range that separated the coastal city of Starspell and their destination.

Leaving was bittersweet for Azure. She looked forward to finding a place they could live more freely, but there was so much in Starspell she wanted to experience yet wouldn't get to. It had been so long since she had been in the human lands, and she hated to leave such a beautiful place so soon, but they didn't have a choice. She held onto that truth as Night Step took her further from the Lamalis Sea and deeper into forbidden territory.

Elios' arm was warm around her waist as he held her close, steadying her as the horses trotted along the cobblestone path. The strength of his body behind her brought a sense of safety she wasn't used to. So, although worry about their futures cycled through her mind, she leaned into that strength and watched the building rears as they passed by.

With no pedestrians or shoppers behind the businesses they passed, it was easy to leave the city in relative secrecy. Occasionally, they passed a woman sweeping, or a man loading vegetables onto a cart, but no one paid them any mind. Still, Elios made sure her face remained hidden beneath a hooded cloak as they traveled, Markos doing the same for Ocevia.

The two fugitive mermaids were not the only ones who hid their appearances, however. The men donned identical cloaks before they set off, their faces shadowed by the hoods to hide their identities from the people they passed. Although the cloaks were warm under the afternoon sun, Azure knew she would be grateful for it when the sun slumbered and left the world in cold darkness once more.

The cobblestone roads of the city changed into a dirt one, leading them into the mountain pass. With the city behind her, the tension in Azure's shoulders relaxed a little.

"How long until we reach Ceveasea?" Azure leaned back against Elios' chest, tipping her head up to look at him. She was rewarded with a kiss on the temple, sending a shiver of electricity across her body as the hand on her waist moved to her hip.

"It should only take a few days, depending on the length of our stops, and on the weather." The hand on her hip began to draw idle circles on the fabric of her trousers, but she felt his touch burn on her skin. "There are some camps and large cave systems in the mountains. There'll be ample places to rest along the way, but I know we need to keep water in consideration for you and Ocevia. Also, I don't want to be stuck in the pass overnight without cover."

The reminder of what would happen if they didn't wet their tails every twenty-four hours made Azure's stomach churn. Part of her wanted to tempt fate, just see what would happen if she didn't abide by the rule, to see if Miris had lied to them to keep them in the sea, but she wasn't brave enough, or stupid enough, to try. She nodded and closed her eyes as a cool breeze swept past, chilling the sweat that had accumulated under her hood.

Hoof steps grew louder as Markos approached, his horse moving in step beside them. "Any ideas where you want to stop tonight, Brother?" Markos asked. His arm was wrapped around Ocevia's waist, and the blond was grinning from ear-to-ear. Azure hoped her friend didn't move too fast, though she didn't have room to lecture her, because she'd done the same thing with Elios. So far, she didn't regret her decision, even though she had new questions about what he did for a living. Both she and her best friend had gone without real physical and emotional connections for so long, for their entire lives really, so could anyone truly blame them for taking the opportunity when it presented itself? Not that she cared if anyone did.

Elios looked to the sky before turning back to Markos. "We need a place we can defend, somewhere with a water source, before sundown. You know the creatures that roam these lands at night. I don't want to be vulnerable once we lose the protection of daylight."

Markos nodded, the hard set of his jaw showing he understood the risks, and the creatures Elios spoke of. Just imagining the kinds of bloodthirsty beasts that prowled the mountains at night filled Azure's mouth with a familiar sour taste.

Markos scanned their group before addressing Elios again. "There's a camp about five hours from here. Maybe less if we pick up the pace."

"Let's try to get there before sundown," Elios responded.

Markos nodded and lifted the reins, encouraging his horse to pick up speed. The rest of their group acted accordingly, without any verbal directives. Elios' pulled Azure closer, nestling her between his thighs, his biceps tightening around her as he urged Night Step into a gallop.

Chapter Fifteen
Arcane River Tribe

Exhausted and sore from riding, they reached the camp just before the sun disappeared beyond the horizon. Set against massive rocky cliffs with caves scattered along the mountain's base, the camp was not devoid of people, as Azure had expected. Instead, dozens formed a make-shift community, tucked away from the cities and towns of nearby kingdoms. Many people, including children, congregated around an enormous bonfire as an entire animal carcass roasted above it. Azure couldn't determine the type of animal, but the scent made her mouth water.

Markos moved ahead, dismounting, and handing the reins to Dimitrius before walking over to speak with one of the natives, a large man armed with a spear, whose braids fell down the length of his back.

"This is the Arcane River Tribe." Elios whispered into her ear. "Markos is getting permission from a tribal elder for us to stay for the night. We'll be safe here, and there's a river that flows through the cave system for you and Ocevia to... soak."

His hesitation to mention their tails made her curious, but the kiss he placed beneath her ear was distracting. "A river inside the caves?"

She felt him nod, his hair tickling her cheek. "A warm one. It's fed by a hot spring."

Mention of a hot spring brought flashbacks of their nights in the island cave to her mind. She closed her eyes, enjoying the memory. When she reopened them, Markos and the tribal elder were approaching the group. Their faces were unreadable, but she hoped the tribe would approve their stay for the night. The prospect of them setting back out into the mountain pass after dark sent a chill sweeping over her, Elios' vague warning about bloodthirsty creatures echoing in her mind.

"We can stay," Markos said, motioning to the man at his side. "This is a tribal elder, Great Protector." The large man nodded once and walked away without a word. "Great Protector said we can take the caves at the far end." Markos pointed to the right side of the cliffs. "There are a few rooms inside and water for drinking and bathing. He exchanged gold for the night."

Elios nodded, motioning to the rest of their party as Markos rejoined Ocevia on their horse. As they made for the caves assigned to them, they received a few glances from those lingering by the fire, but most of the tribe paid them no mind as they passed by.

"Elios," Azure murmured. She leaned in closer as he moved a wayward hair behind her ear.

"Hmm?"

"You mentioned creatures that made traveling at night too dangerous. I was wondering... what kinds of creatures?"

His arms tightened around her, almost reflexively, and that scared her more than anything. "There are beings that hunt in these mountains. They drain the blood from their victims and leave the dead for other, lesser predators to consume. They are the ones we avoid at night."

Ice filled her veins as every shadow took on a sinister edge. She gripped the saddle horn tighter. "That sounds like a nightmare."

He held her so tight it almost hurt. "They are, but we'll do our best to never come across them. Don't worry. As long as we make camp before sunset, we'll be safe."

They passed a larger cave that was closed off with a wooden gate as they made their way to their temporary lodgings. Azure just barely recognized the shapes of horses inside. Markos led them to the gate and a tribe member approached to take their mounts. With the creatures said to stalk the mountain pass, there was no wonder why they kept their horses under such protection.

For the first time in hours, Azure left the saddle—with Elios' help. Her lower extremities were stiff and achy from the long ride, and she was relieved to get the blood flowing again. The travel party gathered their belongings, handing over the reins to the man watching the animals.

Azure stretched her stiff legs while they waited for the stable hand to lead all four horses away. Once the last animal was collected, they headed for their caves. Ocevia approached as soon as Markos lifted her from their horse. To Azure's delight, her friend wore a broad smile.

"Markos said there is a heated river inside!" The excitement in the blond mermaid's voice was undeniable. Azure grinned.

"Are you having fun? You seem awfully happy."

Ocevia smacked her on the arm, but the flush in her cheeks said it all. "Yes. I am, actually. Markos smells so good, and he's been such a gentleman. Plus, he's *really* handsome."

Azure threaded her fingers through Ocevia's as the men led the way. "Well, I'm glad you've enjoyed his company since you were stuck on a horse with him all day. Do you still want to ride with him tomorrow?"

Ocevia practically skipped toward the cave, her eyes sparkling. "Of course, I'm going to ride with him again. I'm *going* to make him my husband."

Fighting back an eye roll, Azure squeezed Ocevia's hand. She didn't want her friend to get her heart broken, but it wasn't her right to tell the blond who she could pursue, or who she could love.

There was no way to know what would happen between those two, just like there was no way to know what the future held for her and Elios. She just hoped, if or when the time came, that Markos would be as accepting of Ocevia's mermaid nature as Elios was with hers.

Standing in the way of what Ocevia wanted was something Azure could never bring herself to do. The blond had already been denied so much in her life, and Azure refused to be another barrier to Ocevia's happiness.

Instead, when they arrived at the cave entrance, Azure squeezed her friend's hand one more time and then ushered her back off to Markos' side with a word of caution.

"You don't have to tell him about... us... if you're not ready. You can always wait until he sleeps to soak *properly*. Don't feel pressured."

Ocevia hugged her tight before joining the shaggy-haired man, who, to Azure's relief, smiled as her friend approached. She smiled to herself as she saw him reach for Ocevia's hand. It was a far cry from the disinterested man they'd met that morning.

The cluster of caves they were assigned to was larger than Azure expected. There was a main room with a firepit, fire already burning within, and multiple doorways to the side that led to the sleeping quarters, a leather screen blocking each entrance. The sulfuric aroma of the hot spring filled the room, and she followed it to the source. A large pool filled the rear of the cave, fed by a stream that snaked through the back of their cavern, leading to their neighbors on both sides.

Azure's hopes of privacy were dashed. The pool was accessible to anyone who occupied the main room. It would be hard to shift without their group seeing, so she hoped Elios had a plan for that.

Ocevia and Markos branched off first, entering the nearest bedroom together. Azure followed Elios into another chamber, setting her belongings next to a stone platform that was covered in fur blankets. She worried about her friend staying with a stranger after only one day, but she'd done the same thing with

Elios. She felt like a hypocrite, and kept having to remind her-self that, no matter how young Ocevia seemed, she was a grown woman who was capable of making her own decisions.

Azure reclined on the stone bed, caressing the silky furs as her lover ducked back into the main chamber. After years of sleep-ing without a blanket, and on cold stone, the luxurious mate-rial made her want to curl up and never leave. Even without a mattress, the thick fur made it the most comfortable bed she'd ever laid on.

Elios opened his mouth to speak as he reentered the room, but his attention waned as he stared at her sprawled across the furs on her stomach. His eyes darkened as he crossed the room in three long strides. Lifting her torso and resting on her elbows, Azure stared over her shoulder at his wicked grin. His facial hair had grown since she'd first pulled him out of the sea, and it gave his handsome face a rugged look that she found irresistible.

His hands landed on her calves, sliding up her legs and lin-gering on her rear before moving higher. Planting his hands on either side of her body, he leaned down to claim her lips, his hard length nestling against her backside as his tongue caressed hers. The delicious kiss, and the promise of more of his touch, made her arch against him. She swirled her hips, grinding her backside against his cock.

When he pulled away, they were both panting.

"Sorry," he said, lifting himself up with one arm and rolling her onto her back with the other, settling himself between her thighs. "I was coming to let you know the others went to get food from the main campfire."

Azure slid her fingers beneath the hem of his tunic, tracing just above the waistband of his trousers as he hovered over her. "And Ocevia?"

"I couldn't pull her away from Markos if I tried. She left with him."

Azure sighed, her desire taking the back burner as she worried about her friend. "I don't want her to get her heart broken."

Elios kissed her forehead. "Markos is a good man. I've known him since we were kids."

"Alright. I guess I'll trust your word since I don't know him. I have one more question though."

"Yes?"

Azure grinned up at him, her fingers slipping beneath his waistband. "You said the others went back to the main fire. That means we won't be disturbed, right?"

Elios' salacious smile grew as he agreed, leaning forward and kissing his way down her neck. When his tongue came back up the column of her throat, her back bowed and she moaned, fisting the blankets as he ground his hips against her.

"Do you like that, Azure? The taste of you drives me wild." Callused fingers slid into her tunic and up her stomach, tracing around the peaks of her breast. Her arching into his touch only seemed to fuel the roving kisses on her neck.

Her responding affirmation was not much more than a breathy groan. Pulling his hand out from under her tunic, Elios rose to his knees and made quick work of the ties that held her tunic shut, pulling it off and tossing it to the ground. Azure reached for the ties on his trousers, but Elios swatted her hand away. "Not yet. Be patient."

She growled, frustrated, but laid back as he slid back over her, taking her nipple into the warmth of his mouth and caressing the other with his palm. Her body throbbed with need at his sensual touch, but when she reached for his trousers again, he twisted out of her reach and chuckled against her skin.

"You're so demanding tonight, Azure."

"And you're so teasing tonight."

His hand traced from her breast over her stomach until he reached the mound between her legs, cupping her through her trousers. Her hips bucked against him at the maddening pressure. "I'm not trying to tease you, love. I'm just trying to give you pleasure."

No matter what he claimed, he *was* teasing her, and she couldn't take much more. She writhed beneath him as he kissed along her chest and stomach, silently begging him to go lower. He knew exactly what he was doing to her. His smirk said it all. Elios replaced his hand with the bulge in his trousers again, rubbing his hard length against her center. Their clothes were maddening.

"If you want to make me feel good tonight, take off your trousers and give me what I want. Save this for another night. I'm ready *now*."

Her words seemed to shatter his self-control and his mouth collided with hers in a dominating kiss that made her head spin as his hips smashed against her again, rubbing his hardness against her so roughly that her moan was almost a scream.

She yanked at the ties of his trousers again, and this time, he didn't move out of her way. Instead, he helped her. They hastily ripped off each other's clothes as their tongues danced. As soon as the last barrier was cast aside, he slammed into her, and this time there was no mistaking her scream of ecstasy. They may have heard her from the main fire, but she didn't care. Passion raged between them, and they made love hard, both reaching their releases quickly before collapsing into a breathless heap of limbs and sweat.

Azure's stomach interrupted the lust-filled aftermath, growling like a starving beast, and she couldn't help but laugh. Elios kissed her once more before rising from the bed and offering her a hand. "Let's get you something to eat."

It was a suggestion she couldn't argue with. She dug through the nest of discarded clothing that littered the floor, cleaning up and dressing quickly. "Do you think I'll be able to bathe and soak my tail tonight? I feel disgusting after hours of travel." Not to mention the stickiness between her thighs, but she kept that to herself.

Azure admired Elios' chiseled form as he pulled on the same trousers she'd just desperately ripped off, fighting with the ties on her tunic as she stared. It had been so long since she'd worn human clothing and being distracted didn't help. "You'll be able to bathe later. I'll talk to the guys and make sure they all give you and Ocevia the privacy you need, unless Ocevia decides to tell Markos."

The thought made Azure cringe, but she knew she was just being overprotective. Her friend was an adult, but still, her entire life had always centered around being a mermaid and all the curse entailed. She'd never learned about living like a human woman, with human relationships.

"I guess she'll have to if she intends to pursue him. I just hope he handles it as well as you did. I know it's still soon, but we're in a dire situation. It feels like death is looming over us at every turn. I don't blame her for wanting a companion."

Elios' arms wrapped around her after she pulled her trousers on, squeezing her gently. "Don't worry so much. I promise, Markos is one of the good ones. Some of us have heard stories of mermaids in the Lamalis Sea. Of course, I didn't believe them before, but it's hard to deny when you come face-to-face with a woman who has a tail. He'll take it well, even if I need to speak with him."

Azure nodded, not wholly convinced. There was no way to predict how anyone would handle their truth, but Marcos was tasked with protecting them. Undertaking such a long journey, protecting two foreign women with no explanation, to help his friend? That said something about his character, so she would have to have faith that he was who Elios said he was.

They joined the others at the bonfire just as the roasted animal was being carved and handed out on bone plates. Settled near a large group of tribespeople, not too far from the fire, it was obvious, from the sound of red-haired Dimitris, that there was more being passed around than just meat.

Each member of their party held a bone mug and seemed to be enjoying themselves, some more than others. Dimitris greeted them first, throwing his arms around the pair in a group hug that was far more enthusiastic than the moment warranted. Azure giggled, patting him on the back.

"You guys have to try this drink the Arcane people brewed. Stronger than any whiskey I've ever had." His voice was loud, and she was certain it carried to the other side of the massive fire.

Elios took the mug from his friend and squeezed him on the shoulder. "You need to slow down, Brother, or you'll retch right off your horse come morning."

Dimitris raised his finger, looking ready to argue, but seemed to change his mind and nodded instead. "You're probably right, Brother. I think I need to eat some of that bear."

"Bear?"

The thought of eating a bear made Azure queasy, but she was too starved to turn it down. Just because she'd never tried it didn't mean it wasn't good. She and Elios headed for the food line, trailing behind the swaying Dimitris, who had certainly over-indulged before their arrival.

The Arcane people were quite generous, or maybe Markos paid with more gold than she'd thought. Elios and Azure's plate was filled to the brim, and as the scent filled her nose, she found herself not caring about the kind of animal she was about to consume. Her stomach rumbled as they joined their group beside the fire.

Ocevia, to Azure's surprise, was cuddled up against Markos, sitting on a giant log with Aris and eight tribespeople, both male and female. Markos' arm was wrapped around her friend's waist as they laughed at a story Aris was telling.

No one seemed as intoxicated as Dimitris, but it was clear they'd missed quite a party while otherwise engaged. Not that Azure minded. If given the chance to do it all over again, she still would have stayed back in the cave with her lover.

Elios squeezed in next to Markos and pulled her onto his lap, reaching around to take a piece of roasted meat from their plate.

Azure sipped from the bone mug Markos handed to her, but the liquor burned her throat. After how drunk she'd gotten from the wine, she didn't want to repeat the same mistake. She offered the drink to Elios and smiled as a tribal woman gave her a mug of water. Already pitying Dimitris for the headache he would wake up with, she shared the water with him.

They sat around the fire for hours, listening to the stories of the tribespeople, and Aris' stories of sailing the sea. The long-haired male had experienced so much in his life, more than Azure could ever imagine. She watched as Ocevia laughed while snuggling into Markos' side. The shaggy-haired man seemed quite smitten with her friend. They weren't overly affectionate in front of the group, other than the cuddles, but it was still clear they had chosen each other, even if only for the moment. Azure was happy for her friend. If Ocevia could experience love in her life, or even lust, it was worth the risk of heartbreak. It didn't stop Azure from hoping Markos wouldn't hurt her friend, though.

She found herself imagining the future, and whether she and Ocevia could settle somewhere on the land with Elios and Markos and live as humans. It was an impossible dream, but her desire to live that future was strong. She was setting her heart on something so unlikely that she decided to tuck the fantasy away for later and focused on the present. For that moment, she needed to take things as they came.

By the time they went to bed that night, after the mermaids bathed and soaked their tails privately, Azure could barely keep her eyes open. She didn't even dwell on the next leg of their journey as she fell into a deep, dreamless sleep.

Chapter Sixteen
SECRETS REVEALED

Heavy rain and harsh winds greeted them at first light, making traveling impossible. Their plans dissolved in the torrential downpour, putting them behind schedule. Elios believed the Arcane camp was safe to remain in for another day, but the fear of Miris' people catching up to them was very real.

Still, the weather was too harsh, and even if the storm broke later in the day, it would be too risky to leave. If they couldn't make it to another camp before nightfall, they would be at the mercy of the bloodsucking beasts Elios had warned them about.

The main bonfire was moved into a large central chamber that could be reached by traversing the tunnels that ran through the cliff side. Aris called through the leather sheet that sectioned off their room, letting them know breakfast was being served by the displaced fire, but with the storm raging outside, there was no reason to rush from bed that morning.

Elios echoed back his thanks before nuzzling his face into the crook of Azure's neck. She leaned her head against his, the warmth he radiated along with the luxury of the fur bedding lulling her back to the land of dreams. Sleeping in Elios' firm embrace was something Azure looked forward to every night and something she could no longer live without. The time they'd spent together was short, but life-changing, and she knew he was the only man for her.

Eventually, the smell of food wafting through the tunnels and into their cave pulled them from the bed, and their group joined the tribespeople at the main fire. Azure sat between Elios' legs; his arms wrapped around her. The cave blocked most of the fierce winds, even though the screen covering the exit had to be removed, since it kept falling over. The strong flames were deliciously warm, chasing away the grim atmosphere the weather caused, as they nibbled on dried bear meat.

It seemed like the entire tribe had gathered in the cavern that morning, sharing stories and chatting amongst themselves. Azure gazed around the space, admiring all the unfamiliar faces who surrounded her, until she landed on Ocevia. Her friend sat between Markos' legs, just as she had with Elios, a radiant smile on her lips. Their fingers were interlaced, and Markos held her tight, leaning forward to whisper in her ear. The blond's cheeks were stained pink, but her cheerful expression never faltered. They looked comfortable together, close even, but Azure still worried for her friend, just like she worried for herself. Their untrained hearts were so fragile.

If they were captured and returned to the sea, even if Elios and Markos escaped Miris' clutches, she knew the loss would destroy her, and she hoped Ocevia could escape that. Just the thought of having to leave Elios behind opened a pit in her stomach, so she did her best to push the thoughts away and focused on how happy Ocevia looked instead. Living in the moment was all they had, and the fear of pain didn't outweigh the importance of happiness.

Dimitris arrived later than the rest, undoubtedly needing to sleep off the excessive amount of liquor he'd consumed the night before. He didn't say much as he plopped down beside Aris and guzzled water. He looked awful, with bloodshot eyes, bagged and rimmed with dark circles, and a tangled nest of ginger hair sticking up in odd directions. A woman handed a strip of dried meat to him and encouraged him to eat something to settle his stomach, but he didn't bite into it right away, seeming to have a difficult enough time holding the water down. His hangover made Azure glad the rain held them hostage, because he certainly needed a day of rest.

With the unchanging surroundings, she lost track of how long they'd sat around the fire. Time didn't seem to mean much in such an isolated place with people who didn't bend to the rules of modern society. They lived according to their own schedules, structuring their days around their food sources and the weather. Their traditions were shared through oral storytelling and revolved around the deeds of others. Living in such a tribe intrigued Azure. She wouldn't have minded living in such a close-knit community. Though they were not all related, the tribespeople treated each other and their guests like family.

After listening to tribal stories until her rear grew numb from the stone floor, and nibbling on dried meat and roasted root vegetables, Azure was quite content. It was not yet bedtime, but with the storm clouds blotting out the sun, she could hardly hold her eyes open as she and Elios returned to the privacy of their cave.

With the others still at the communal fire, it was the perfect time for her and Elios to bathe and for her to soak her tail. They each grabbed a set of clean clothes and listened for signs of anyone approaching. With no voices coming from the tunnels, they decided it was safe enough and undressed, slipping into the warm water. Shifting into her mermaid form, Azure let out a happy sigh as the heat enveloped her.

Even with the subtle scent of sulfur in the air, the hot spring was an absolute luxury. It was so much more pleasant than the frigid Lamalis Sea.

Cradling Azure from behind, Elios used berries to clean himself before running his hands into her hair, massaging the soap substitute against her scalp. His touch made her shiver, and she closed her eyes, leaning against him. Nothing else mattered right then. Her fears and anxieties were washed away by the warm pool as she melted into the powerful body behind her.

Azure was so lost in the moment that she didn't hear the footsteps as Dimitris sauntered into the chamber before she could shift back into her human form. Even in his low-energy state, his mouth fell open as he stared at her iridescent tail, paying no mind to her breasts that were fully exposed above the surface. She froze, unsure of what to do now.

The rest of their party followed behind Dimitris, their footsteps approaching from the tunnel, but he didn't move from the tunnel's entrance, his eyes remaining wide. Elios pulled her behind him without a word, blocking her with his body. His touch released her from her statuesque state, allowing her to shift, but it was too late. Dimitris already knew what she was, and it sent the air fleeing from her lungs.

"You will say *nothing*." Elios hissed, leaving no room for argument. Dimitris was his friend, but his tone said protecting Azure's identity was more important. Dimitris nodded, but still didn't move. Still unsure how to respond to the intrusion and her vulnerability, Azure folded her arms over her bare chest. The rest of the group walked around him, and her heart sank as she took in their expressions. They saw. *They all saw.*

Markos didn't appear surprised, and Ocevia's eyes were downcast as she fidgeted with the hem of her tunic. Aris rubbed the back of his neck, staring at a fixed point above their heads. Azure appreciated his consideration for her state of undress.

Elios tugged a hand through his wet hair, his agitation clear. "Make a fire and wait for us. Looks like we all need to talk."

The others shuffled away as Azure gazed into the distance, her eyes seeing nothing. She wished they'd never entered the bathing pool at all. If only she had shifted back as soon as her tail was wet. It was only a matter of time before the men they traveled with learned the truth, but she wasn't ready to reveal her nature just yet. Her skin crawled, and her legs were twitchy, like they were ready to spring into action and carry her away, but there was nowhere to run. Elios turned and crushed her to his chest, his firm hold soothing her anxiousness.

"They won't say anything," he murmured into her hair. She hated putting him at odds with his friends, his allies, and hoped his men wouldn't turn on them. Whatever his men signed up for when they'd joined them, it wasn't to put their lives on the line for two fugitive mermaids who were being hunted by an evil goddess and her minions.

She blew out a slow breath. "This is bad, isn't it?" Warm hands rubbed up and down her back as she clung to him like he was her only lifeline.

He squeezed her gently and pulled away, meeting her eyes. "It's going to be okay; I promise. My men are loyal to me."

Azure squeezed her eyes shut and took a deep breath, nodding. "Are you ever going to tell me what you and these men do? I know you're more than a traveler on the hunt for adventure."

Elios rubbed her back one last time and stared over her shoulder at the others. "I'll explain everything by the fire. Let's get out and dress before they come looking for us."

CHAPTER SEVENTEEN
THE CIRCLE

J ust as Elios requested, the rest of their group waited around the firepit. Aris stoked the fire that flared to life quickly. Markos looked completely at ease, leaning back with his legs outstretched and his arm snug around Ocevia's waist. He nodded at the pair in greeting as they neared. Dimitris' shocked expression was gone, making Azure wonder if they'd talked amongst themselves before she and Elios arrived.

With her heart thundering in her ears, she approached the group with her hand white knuckled in Elios'. He guided her to the vacant side of the fire and dropped to the floor, pulling her onto his lap. His closeness eased her nerves ever so slightly.

"I guess I should give you all an explanation," Elios began. The rest of the room remained silent as he spoke, eyes unblinking as they waited for him to continue. "We're not traveling with human women, as you now know, but I guess I should start at the beginning."

Without hesitation, Elios launched into the story, starting with the shipwreck, moving on to his rescue. He told them of their lives as mermaids, and the details of the curse, even the horrible requirements needed to break it. He held back nothing, telling them why they were running and from whom.

No one spoke as they all listened intently, even Ocevia. Although she'd found them on the island, she didn't know all the details from before Oona and Lucia had attacked them. Aside from their sex life, he shared just about every detail. They remained quiet, but no one looked ready to run in the opposite direction, so Azure took that as a good sign.

When Elios finished speaking, there was a collective exhale in the room, but still no one spoke for several long moments. Aris finally broke the silence.

"So, are Azure and Ocevia intending to stay out of the sea for good?"

It was the question Azure did not have a genuine answer for, though she mulled it over frequently. She would have been happy to never return to the Lamalis Sea, because it was Miris' domain, but she could have also been happy to live near another body of water, spending time within its depths without the obligation to kill. She hated being a mermaid, but she couldn't deny that it was her life, *her curse*. The idea of never swimming in open water again made her oddly uncomfortable.

Elios looked at Azure, deferring to her for the answer. Tucking her damp hair behind her ear, she glanced at the others as they awaited her response.

"I'm not sure, but I know I don't want to be within the reach of Miris. If she finds us, she'll kill me, and Elios, too. So, the farther we get from her lair, the safer we'll be. Ocevia has never disobeyed the Sea Goddess before, not like I have, so she might survive... after being tortured for running away."

She looked at the blond female and saw Markos squeeze her gently and place a kiss on her temple. Any question of whether Markos and Ocevia were romantically involved faded away, as well as whether he already knew her true nature. His lack of a reaction said it all.

"I won't let that happen," Markos said. "Even if I need to take her to another continent, Ocevia will not spend another moment in slavery. Not while I'm still drawing breath."

A small smile spread across Ocevia's face, but Azure knew her well enough to know that her friend was uncertain about her future. After spending nearly her entire life as a mermaid, she didn't have the ability to imagine life as a human, even if she'd fallen in love with a human man.

Azure could tell Markos meant what he said, though. He obviously cared for Ocevia and prioritized her safety and freedom over himself. Elios vouched for his friend's character, and she found no reason to doubt him.

Markos cleared his throat, continuing. "But I do have a confession to make..." He paused, running his fingers down Ocevia's cheek. "I already knew they were mermaids. The tribal elder, Great Protector, told me when we arrived. I figured Elios already knew, figured it was why we were running. I didn't want to say anything, out of protection for Ocevia and Azure, not until Elios said something first." Markos turned to face his friend; whose face was etched with uncertainty. "I was going to talk to you about it, Brother, but I was waiting until we got somewhere more secure."

Azure looked at Elios' handsome face, waiting for him to react to Markos' admission, waiting for him to explain who he and his men were. Even though her secret was out, the worry lines creasing his forehead told her Elios wasn't looking forward to sharing his own, nor was he particularly happy with Markos' omission.

"I would have said something once we arrived in Ceveasea for the same reason you didn't speak up, Markos. It's not that I didn't trust you, Aris, or Dimitris. We've been through a lot together, and I trust all three of you with my life. But I knew what they were wasn't relevant to our mission, and I couldn't chance anyone finding out who could put them at risk. Anyone at this camp could turn them over for a bit of coin. It was best to hold on to their secret for a while, at least until we got to a safe-house." Clearing his throat, Elios squeezed Azure tighter against his chest. "I suppose there is more I need to explain, at least to Azure and Ocevia." Markos' eyebrows furrowed, but he didn't interrupt. Ocevia sat straighter, clearly interested. Elios turned back to face Azure. "I told you I've spent my life traveling. That wasn't a lie, but it wasn't the whole truth either." He paused, rubbing the back of his neck. "You asked what The Circle was back at the tavern. Well, Aris, Dimitris, Markos, and I are part of that group. Our mission is to rescue slaves and smuggle them away to the lands where they can live free."

Azure didn't know how to respond to his confession, but it made sense. The way he'd tried to comfort her over her guilt for taking lives, the way he insisted Miris was at fault and not her. It all made sense. He'd spent his life, risked his life, to rescue slaves. It made her love him even more. "And Vasso?"

Elios nodded. "Yes, Vasso and his wife are also part of The Circle, but their roles are different from ours, although no less dangerous. Their inn is used to house freed slaves, and ourselves, when we pass through. It also serves as a communication hub for members. The rest of us, more than twenty now, this is our lives. Some of us have been doing this since we were teens. Many kingdoms still support slaveholders, their kings even profiting from the trade, but we do our best to rescue who we can."

Azure was silent for a moment, head spinning at the realization of who Elios was. It filled her with admiration for how brave he was, but fear flooded in as well. What he did for a living was more dangerous than she could even fathom and she worried for his safety.

"So, what happens to us now?" Ocevia's voice caught Azure by surprise. She and Elios turned to her friend in unison, but it was Elios who responded.

"Nothing changes from here. We'll leave this camp when the weather clears and make our way through the mountain pass to the city of Ceveasea. If we hear any word of Miris' people snooping around, we'll move further inland. Aris and Dimitris will eventually return to Starspell for their next assignment, but I assume Markos will stay with us." Aris and Dimitris both nodded in confirmation before everyone looked at Markos.

He also nodded, his arms visibly tightening around his lover. "I won't leave Ocevia. There's nothing back in Starspell for me. I can still do my job from inland."

Ocevia melted into Markos as he rubbed her back. She looked more content than Azure had ever seen her, and she looked forward to talking to Ocevia about her budding romance. There was never a reason for them to talk about men before, but this gave them a chance to behave like normal women.

The conversation died after that, and the group disbanded for the night. With their secret out, and the men still willing to protect them, Azure crawled into bed with Elios and slept, less weighing on her shoulders than before.

Chapter Eighteen
THROUGH THE MOUNTAINS

B y the next morning, the storm had cleared, leaving the window for travel wide open. Azure was sure the path would be incredibly muddy, but that wasn't enough to delay them any longer. The more days they remained stagnant, the likelier Miris' people would find them. So, after thanking the Arcane tribe for their hospitality and a long series of goodbyes, the group readied their horses, loaded their belongings, and set out for the city of Ceveasea.

Everyone wore hooded cloaks again, to obscure their identities should they come across anyone along the mountain pass. Azure wondered if she would be forced to hide her face until her dying day. No matter how far she ran, Miris would never let her go, hunting her until she drew her last breath. There was no end in sight. The Sea Goddess' reach was limitless.

The rain left behind a chill in the air, and Azure wrapped the cloak tightly around herself as she sat cradled between Elios' thighs, thankful for the clothing Vasso and his wife had supplied. She and Ocevia had soaked their tails briefly before leaving, not knowing if they would have another chance that day, but now that they trudged through the cold and toward their next destination, she wished they'd have taken their time in the hot spring. Elios said they should reach the border city before nightfall, but there was no guarantee. She hoped he was right. Not only did Azure have no interest in seeing the murderous nocturnal creatures Elios had told her about, but she also wanted nothing more than to curl up in his arms by a blazing fire.

The path they took was said to be incredibly dangerous, overrun with bandits who attacked and robbed unsuspecting travelers. She was on high alert, keeping her head on a swivel as they moved forward, hoping to not see any threats. She'd already had enough danger to last a lifetime.

As their horses trotted down the muddy mountain path, Azure's mind began to wander, and she thought about her sister frequently. What was Daneliya's life like? Did she still live in Thatia? She didn't know who took care of her sister after she had been cursed by Miris. All she knew about the girl now was that she was nearly eleven years old. They were each other's only remaining family, which was worrisome. She hoped her sister wasn't being raised in an orphanage or given to a family that mistreated her. Azure should be by her side, and she felt the loss of her sister every day. Missing so much of Daneliya's life tugged at her heart, threatening to tear it apart. Even in the rare instances when she felt content, or a little joy, that grief was still a shadow looming over her, threatening to consume her. Having Elios in her life made her happy, but he didn't replace her sister. His love and companionship didn't fill the void that losing Daneliya had created, but he softened the sharp edges.

"We'll stop for a break soon." Breath warmed her cheek as Elios spoke into her ear. "Are you hungry?"

She shrugged, her nerves rattling in her stomach. "I'll eat. How much further do we have to go?"

He looked ahead as though he could map out their route in his mind. With his travel experience, he probably could. "I would say we have about five hours left, but I'd like to make better time. We shouldn't stop for long. I don't want to be caught in these mountains overnight."

Visions of massive bloodsucking beasts flooded her mind. She didn't want to be caught overnight, either. Always the pessimist, the worst-case scenarios plagued her. "What happens if we don't make it?"

Elios kissed her cheek. "Even if we can't make it before we lose daylight, we'll be okay. There are plenty of caves along the pass. We can bunk down and light fires to keep what dwells in the night away. I would just prefer to avoid that if we can, but I won't let anything happen to you either way. Don't worry."

His protectiveness sent flutters straight to her core. She knew Elios would take care of her, no matter what. She just hoped there never came a time where he *couldn't* keep her safe. She didn't want him to get hurt, nor blame himself if something happened to her.

Reassured, Azure nestled further into his chest and took in the scenery. Plant life was sparse, though stubborn patches of grass sprouted up through the rocky terrain. Jagged peaks stabbed the sky at astounding heights, lending a menacing edge to the atmosphere. It made her wonder what vicious threat hid within the dark hollows that littered the mountains and whether any eyes followed them as they passed. She shuddered at the thought.

They slowed the horses to a stop as a stream intersected their path, a patch of grass along its bank perfect for the animals to graze. The stream wasn't very wide, but it was enough for them to refill their canteens. Azure and Ocevia took the time to wet their tails in the stream before eating. It hadn't been long since they last soaked, but with no idea when they would have access to water again, it seemed like a good opportunity to restart their twenty-four-hour clock.

Lunch was dried bear meat from the Arcane camp. Azure had yet to decide if it was tasty because it wasn't dried fish, or if she actually liked the flavor.

The group sat together as they ate, bonding amongst themselves. With no more secrets between them, the air felt lighter. Elios and Dimitris sharpened their swords with similar stones as they told stories of their past rescues, the former periodically taking the bites of food Azure offered to him. Ocevia braided Aris' waist-length hair and Markos leaned back on his elbows, watching the blond mermaid with lovesick eyes. The golden-haired man had his eyes closed, seeming to enjoy Ocevia's ministrations.

"Have you spoken to Kimon recently?" Dimitris asked, after recalling a particularly dangerous mission that included the member of their group who lived in Ceveasea.

Elios stopped sharpening his blade. "About six months ago. Why? Any recent developments?"

Dimitris huffed a laugh. "Do you remember the woman he was seeing? What was her name? Emilia, maybe? Well, our old friend, Kimon, got her pregnant. Word is they've since married."

Elios chuckled and slid the sharpening stone against his sword again. "I say good for him. We should all be so lucky to have a good woman to come home to." He reached out and squeezed Azure's hand, bringing rosy warmth to her cheeks. "I know that I feel like the luckiest man alive. Once I get my lady to a safe place, all will be right in the world."

Dimitris laughed as he nodded. "I hope to be just as lucky one day, Brother."

Elios patted his friend on the shoulder before standing and stretching out his back. "Well, we should get back on the move. I don't want these ladies out in the cold mountains after dark."

Returning to their saddles, the group set off in the direction that would take them farther from the sea, and farther from Miris.

After crossing the stream, the pass became rockier as they climbed in elevation, preparing to cross the highest point of their journey. Ceveasea was landlocked in the valley of the Avronis Mountains, on the border of Avrearyn and the inland kingdom of Dekresian. Azure didn't know much about Dekresian, but excitement at seeing such a faraway place brewed inside her. She wondered what the people were like, how the cities and towns looked.

"Is Ceveasea in the kingdom of Avrearyn or Dekresian?" Azure leaned back against Elios' chest so he could hear her voice over the wind that had steadily picked up as they traveled. The hand on her thigh rubbed lazy patterns against the cloth of her trousers.

"Technically, it's part of the Kingdom of Dekresian, but it is claimed by both since it's directly on the border." The caresses to her thigh moved dangerously higher, and she squirmed in the saddle as her belly clenched. "Dekresian outlawed slavery a decade ago. Their king, Tamer of the Fire, was a slave until he escaped as a teen. Because of the kingdom's stance, it's often our destination when shuttling those we've rescued and smuggled out to safety."

The thought of a kingdom opposed to slavery brought a lightness to Azure's chest that she welcomed with open arms. She closed her eyes as Elios nuzzled her neck, her core throbbing from his maddening touches.

"Do any of the kingdoms know what Miris is doing?" She already knew the answer. Miris was but another god the people acknowledged but didn't truly believe in. Elios shook his head.

"Just as mermaids, Miris is a myth to most, real to very few. There are rumors, but most people take them as legends and nothing more. If every story was to be believed, our world would be filled with magical creatures, creatures who do a very good job hiding among the masses. But..." He kissed her again, his lips tender against her jaw. "Since mermaids are real, who knows how many of the others are real as well?"

CHAPTER NINETEEN
WAITING.
WATCHING.
STALKING.

Although the sun had returned to her resting place for the night, leaving them in moonlit darkness, the group didn't set up camp. With the illumination of the city just over the next ridge, Elios thought it best to continue at a brisk pace instead of taking their chances in a cave. It was not a straightforward decision for him to make, with risks either way, but an hour of traveling after dark seemed safer than an entire night spent in the wilderness.

The city was so close, but still so far away. Maybe it was because the horses were tired, or maybe it was because the sway of the saddle made her eyes heavy, but the city lights never seemed to grow closer as they traveled. Night wrapped around them like a suffocating blanket as they headed through the last set of peaks that framed the pass, and the mountains grew eerily silent.

Elios slowed their horse and placed his hand on his sword's hilt, scanning their surroundings. Azure didn't know what he was looking for, but the fierce look in his eyes made her pulse thunder. The other men slowed their mounts as well, eyes searching for a hidden threat.

Azure forgot how to breathe as Elios shoved the reins into her hands and wrapped a protective arm around her waist while pulling his sword from its scabbard with the other. She knew little of how to control a horse. Before being cursed, she only ever saw the animals from a distance, riding them only a few times as a child. Thankfully, their current steed, Dark Heart, kept moving forward without guidance.

A menacing hiss shattered the tense silence. It came from everywhere at once, reverberating off the cliffs that flanked them as they continued through the impenetrable darkness. Dark Heart's steps faltered, his tail twitching violently.

Panic gripped Azure as she searched for the source of the sound. "What was that?" Her voice was only a whisper, but Elios squeezed her tighter as he looked at his men and nodded. The other three men held their swords at the ready. Azure couldn't see Ocevia, but she could hear her friend's rapid breathing, or maybe it was her own. She didn't know which. Dimitris whistled, jerking his head to the left. Something was there, hidden in the shadows. *Watching. Waiting. Stalking.*

Time stood still as the loud snap of wings unfurling boomed around them. Azure cowered against Elios' chest as Aris rushed to their side and swung his blade at the creature, missing his mark. Something dark billowed in her peripheral vision, and the creature melted into the night again. Chattering sounds echoed around them, unlike anything she'd ever heard before. She didn't know what the creature was, and she couldn't sense where they were coming from or how many there were. Every noise rebounded off the stone, making it impossible to identify if there was one threat or one hundred.

Another hiss preceded a hard flap of wings, their only warning before the dark creature flew at them again, swooping down in front of Dark Heart. Elios' sword caught it, and it screamed, the sound piercing. Azure covered her ears instinctively, trying to protect her eardrums. The beast didn't fall. Instead, it retreated again, flying upward until the dark sky masked it.

It was too dark out, and the creature was far too fast for Azure to make out its shape, but the men of The Circle clearly knew what they were up against. Elios let go of her and pulled on the reins she held, digging his feet in and sending Dark Heart into a run. He kissed her neck and whispered he loved her before his warmth disappeared from her back.

For a horrifying moment, Azure thought he'd jumped off the galloping horse, sacrificing himself. She whipped around, but before she could scream his name, she saw him.

Elios stood on the saddle behind her, somehow balancing on the horse's back, with his blade held out in front of him, His boots snapped into shoe holds on the saddle that she'd never noticed before. Rapid movement caught her eye, and she twisted her head to find Aris standing on his saddle as well. Her breath caught in her throat as she watched the men hold steady atop their racing mounts, like they'd done this their entire lives. Dimitris stood just like the other two, and she watched in awe and horror, praying none of them got hurt.

Dimitris whistled just before another hiss echoed through the pass. Only seconds later, the creature descended on them again. In a swoop, it knocked Aris off his horse, and Azure cried out as their friend crashed to the ground with a sickening thud, his horse moving forward without him. She stared at his unmoving form as Dark Heart continued to dash forward. Her chest cleaved in two at the realization that his death was her fault. He lost his life protecting her and Ocevia. A broken sob escaped her lips.

A black creature landed beside their fallen friend, looming over him. It was as tall as a man with... Azure strained to make out the beast and gasped. Their flying attacker was human, or at least it *looked* like a human, aside from its massive wings. Its chalky hands reached for Aris.

Dimitris dropped back onto his saddle and jerked the reins, forcing his horse to turn around. The animal dashed toward the creature, slowing down in time for its rider to jump off. With a furious swing of his sword, their red-haired companion severed the neck of Aris' attacker before it even noticed he had approached. Its head hit the ground, rolling to a stop by the horse's hoof. Azure watched, hoping against all odds that Aris would move, or show a sign of life, any sign, but an enraged shriek from directly above pulled her attention to Elios.

Another humanoid monster swooped down in front of her, and Elios' sword slashed through its center without hesitation. Hot blood splattered the front of her tunic, splashing across her face. Her eyes squeezed shut on impact, and her racing pulse made her dizzy. She didn't dare look again, but she heard the creature's body slam into the cliff to her left.

Elios dropped into the saddle behind her, turning Dark Heart around, and racing back toward Aris and Dimitris. Markos and Ocevia were already with them by the time Azure and Elios returned. Markos held a torch near his friends, shining a light over them on the ground. Relief made tears fall down her gore-spattered face when she caught sight of the man she'd thought was dead speaking to Dimitris. The redhead hovered over him, checking his injuries. All was quiet as Elios dismounted and joined the others, no sign of more horrifying creatures.

"His leg is definitely broken," Dimitris said, his voice more severe than Azure ever heard him produce. "He may have a few broken ribs, too."

Elios crouched beside Aris, discussing plans to get him to the city, while Azure stood sentinel beside him. She'd never felt quite so useless before. All she could do was hope they got him somewhere safe so he could receive attention from a healer.

She looked down and stiffened. The severed head laid at her feet, but it thankfully faced away from her, showing her only its long, bloodied black hair. She was too afraid to look closer, to see its face, knowing its visage would haunt her at night, and she already had enough nightmares that plagued her.

Markos approached with his arm wrapped around Ocevia. He nudged the head with his boot, rolling it back until cold eyes settled on her. Ocevia pressed her face into his chest as Azure gasped.

Two abyssal eyes stared at them with an overpowering animosity, although there was no longer life behind them. Even in the flickering light of the torch, the face was exceedingly pale, almost translucent, but humanoid. Its irises were a deep blood red. Elongated front teeth that looked razor sharp jutted out from its pale gums. Bile rose in Azure's throat as she retreated a step and vomited. The creature wasn't just humanoid. She could feel it in her cursed soul. It had once been human. She didn't know how long it had lived as a monster, or how it had been turned into one, but it used to be just as human as she had been.

"Blood sucking piece of shit," Markos spat, kicking the head into the cliff side. With a splat and a thump, it disappeared from view.

The three of them stood to the side as Aris did his best to sit up. He hissed in pain while Elios and Dimitris helped him to his feet. They supported the injured man's heavy weight, Aris larger than his friends, as the trio headed for Dimitris' horse. Letting go of Ocevia, who quickly grabbed Azure's hand, Markos ran to help lift their friend until he slumped into the saddle.

Aris' arm was wrapped around his middle, supporting his broken ribs, and his jaw was clenched, agony visible in his expression. Dimitris sat behind him, holding onto the injured man while the horse took slow steps forward.

Markos returned for Ocevia and wrapped his arm around her shoulders, leading her to their horse and lifting her onto the saddle. Elios secured the reins of Aris' horse to Dark Heart and helped Azure return to her seat before climbing behind her. The group headed for the safety of the city as the sounds of nocturnal creatures filled the night air once again.

CHAPTER TWENTY
THE DUSTY LANTERN

C hapter 20

They reached Ceveasea with no further attacks. The border city was large, but the streets were deserted. There were no people strolling down the sidewalks or sounds of revelry that met Azure's ears. Aside from the candlelight shining in countless windows, there were no signs of inhabitants. She never saw a human town so devoid of nightlife, even before becoming a mermaid.

"Where is everyone?" Every step their horses took clomped loudly on the silent cobblestone street, setting her teeth on edge.

Elios nodded at the moon sitting high in the sky. "The citizens know what lives just outside their borders, and they're smart enough to avoid them. Unlike Starspell, you won't find many people out in the open here after the sun goes down."

The hair on Azure's arms stood on end as she scanned every building and alley for movement, hoping they would find sanctuary soon. As though the universe aimed to calm her, they turned down a side street and slowed as they approached a gate built into a large stone building. An older man, probably in his fifties, stood on the other side, peering through the bars, and studied them before nodding. He pushed the heavy metal gate open, the groaning hinges echoing in the silence. The group led their horses inside, and the older man closed the gate immediately behind them.

"Staying for long, Elios?" The middle-aged man rasped. He held a lantern high, untethering Aris' horse from Dark Heart, and leading it back into what appeared to be a small stable.

Elios dismounted and helped Azure off their horse. She studied the enclosed courtyard while Elios brought their horse into the stable, tying the steed up near a stack of hay and a water trough. "We're not sure how long this time, Old Man. Do you have a few rooms for us? Say three?"

"Aye," was the man's only response as he readied the stables for the rest of their animals.

Markos helped Ocevia dismount before joining Elios by Dimitris' horse. The three men carefully pulled their friend from the saddle and carried him to a wooden door that led into the main building.

"Is Phaedra inside, Georgios?" Markos reached for the metal door handle, struggling to open it as he helped hold Aris' weight. Their injured friend was barely awake, his eyes rolling back as his head bobbed and swayed, nearly losing the fight to remain alert. The pain looked unbearable, rendering the powerful man helpless, and guilt burrowed deep inside Azure's chest. If he'd never met her, he wouldn't have been suffering.

"Yes. Yes. She's inside." Georgios waved them forward, impatience in his movements. Azure wasn't sure if he disliked company, or just disliked receiving company so late at night.

With her hand in Ocevia's, they followed the men into a storeroom of some sort. The men continued to shuffle carefully down a narrow hallway, illuminated by a lone lantern that cast shadows along the wood-paneled walls. Approaching a set of double doors at the end of the corridor, Elios let the others support Aris' frame as he knocked. Crouching, he slid something under the closed entrance. The doors opened only a moment later.

Black, curly hair hung over the lean face of a middle-aged woman, wide green eyes studying them. When her assessment seemed to be complete, she stepped aside and allowed them to carry their injured friend inside. The men laid Aris on an examination table, careful not to further injure him, but Azure couldn't stop staring at the stranger.

The older woman, who Azure assumed was named Phaedra, clutched the thing Elios had pushed under the door. It was a medallion of some sort. A deep scar ran from the bottom of her right eye to the underside of her cheekbone, like a track of tears left their permanent mark upon her aged skin.

Phaedra moved in close to where their friend laid, taking no time to rip his clothes off with a dagger. "What happened to him?" Her tone was clipped, urgent even. The others huddled around the Aris, but Azure and Ocevia stood back, their faces colored with guilt.

Elios helped her cut Aris' trousers off, throwing the shredded fabric onto the floor. His eyes fluttered as his consciousness came in and out from the pain. "Vampires. A few of the evil beasts attacked us on our way into the city. Knocked him off his horse."

Phaedra shook her head, her expression grim, as she pulled a bottle of swirling liquid from a leather bag. "Was he bitten?"

"No." Elios pried his unconscious friend's mouth open, and the woman used a pipette to squeeze a few drops of the shimmering purple liquid onto his tongue. They worked so efficiently together. Elios acted before Phaedra could issue a command, and Azure wondered how often they'd been in similar situations together before. "He just fell from his horse? His left leg is broken, a few ribs as well. No signs of head trauma, but probably some internal bleeding. A few broken bones wouldn't be enough to make this big man pass out." The healer spoke in an assessing, unemotional way, although her reference to Aris as a "big man" made it sound like the healer knew him well. It was clear she was used to handling such injuries, even those injuries caused by vampire bites. The thought made Azure's blood chill, the image of the creature's face flashing through her mind again.

Markos and Dimitris retreated as Elios and Phaedra worked in tandem. The two men sat on the settee against the far wall, Ocevia joining them and curling into her lover's side as she fought to keep her eyes open. Azure stared at the medallion that laid on the table. Something about it kept drawing her attention as she settled in an unoccupied chair beside the others. The medallion was small and bronze. A broken chain at its center was the only adornment. It was the same symbol tattooed on Elios' chest. Was it his personal identifier, or the symbol of The Circle? It was likely the latter, a fitting mark for a group dedicated to freeing others from their chains.

Aris never moved as Phaedra did a final assessment of his injuries, wrapping his ribs in a tight binding and using a board to set his leg. She washed her hands before pulling keys from her apron.

"You three can carry him into the sickroom across the hall. Then I'll show you to your rooms." Phaedra motioned toward the double doors. "Will you be staying long, Elios?"

Markos and Dimitris moved immediately at the woman's command, grabbing onto Aris along with Elios. "We'll be here for a while. Thank you for your hospitality, Phaedra, and for your discretion." The woman nodded as she shooed them all back into the darkened hallway, following close behind.

After the men got Aris settled in the bed Phaedra pointed to, they were led up a poorly lit staircase and into a corridor lined with guest rooms. Azure assumed the building was some sort of inn, but, with a healer on hand for emergencies, she wasn't certain.

There were more rooms than their party needed, but if any other patrons were there for the night, they were certainly quiet. Dimitris was given a room to himself, leaving two rooms so the two couples could have privacy. Phaedra disappeared after letting them know dinner would be up shortly, her steps creaking on the wooden stairs.

"What is this place?" Stepping in behind Elios, Azure took in the underwhelming space.

The bedchamber was small, lit only by a single gas lantern. It held a double bed, half the size of the one in Starspell, an armoire, and a table only large enough to accommodate two people. The walls were made from the same wood paneling as the downstairs, making the room appear more cramped than it was. The two windows set in the far wall were tiny, making

Azure think they served as an added protection to keep the creatures, vampires Elios had called them, from entering. They sacrificed sunlight for safety.

Only one other door led out of the bedchamber, leading to an equally miniscule bathing room. There was barely any room to maneuver inside, but there was a tub. It relieved some of the tightness in Azure's chest, knowing she and Ocevia could soak their tails discreetly, without fear of anyone else learning about their curse.

"The Dusty Lantern serves many purposes." Elios took so long to respond that she'd forgotten her question altogether. In his defense, however, he had been moving through the two rooms, lighting candles to chase away the shadows, casting the suite in a warm glow. "There is a tavern downstairs, as well as the infirmary and then the inn on the second floor." Elios chuckled. "The tavern patrons usually either end up in the infirmary or in the inn, since no one goes out after dark. It's a good business model. Well, since Phaedra's such a skilled healer." Setting down the last candle, he wrapped his powerful arms around her. Closing her eyes, Azure luxuriated in his warmth, inhaling his delicious scent. "This is usually where we bring those we've freed until we can find them permanent lodgings. My friend, Kimon, has a safe house we typically stay at when we're in the city for an extended period, but I have to get with him to make sure it's vacant. I didn't have a chance to tell him we were coming so he could prepare to receive us."

A knock interrupted their conversation. Placing a kiss on Azure's lips, Elios let go of her so he could cross the room to answer the door. Georgios stood in the hall, holding out a tray of stew, a decanter of wine, and a small loaf of bread. Elios thanked the man as he relieved him of the burden and closed the door, crossing the room and setting the tray on the table.

The rich stew's herby aroma wafted through the air, drawing Azure to the table as her mouth watered. Pulling out her chair, Elios kissed her before taking a set. The care he showed, all that he sacrificed to keep her safe, made her feel loved, even if they hadn't known each other for long. He didn't have to do any of it. His life was in danger because of her. She wouldn't have blamed him if he had abandoned her the moment they'd docked in Starspell, but he remained by her side, unwavering. She never imagined someone would love her the way he did, especially not after Miris took ownership of her soul. It was a dream she never knew to wish for but was grateful it had come true.

Elios sat across from her, serving each of them a bowl of stew and a glass of wine. Azure dug in hungrily, ignoring the heat that scalded her tongue. The hearty chunks of meat and vegetables practically melted in her mouth. After being reintroduced to human food, she never wanted to return to a dried fish diet again. She never wanted to return to a life where it was her only option, a life in the cold sea without Elios' touch to keep her warm. The threat of that was a thought she couldn't handle.

Chapter Twenty-One
CAN WE GET AWAY?

After their exhausting and dangerous day, sleep came quickly for Azure and Elios that night. The chamber's undersized windows allowed little light in, making it far too easy for them to sleep later than usual.

After being nocturnal for years, Azure was surprised at how easily she had adjusted to a normal human routine. Aside from a general threat to their safety, there were no obligations to pull them out of bed, but her body was too used to its normal day-time schedule. Her empty stomach and full bladder threatened to chase her out from beneath the warm blankets if she didn't get up willingly.

Elios' muscular arm was wrapped around her waist when she opened her eyes that morning. Rolling over to admire his sleeping face, which always made her heart flutter, she found him staring back at her instead. His eyes were bright, and his brown hair was so disheveled from sleep that it made him even sexier.

A smile spread across her face at the sight of him and he grinned in response, his blue gaze lightening even more.

"Good morning" His voice was raspy from sleep. Azure felt the depth of it low in her belly.

"Good morning to you."

Pulling her closer to his warm chest, Elios gave her a lingering kiss. "How did you sleep?"

Azure stretched her arms above her head, yawning. "Longer than I needed to, and it was glorious."

Tucking a lock of hair behind her ear, he pressed his lips to her forehead and spoke against her skin, sending shivers down her body. "After everything you've been through, forget about how much you need. You can sleep as much as you *want*, and I'll chase away anyone who tries to disturb you."

She giggled with her cheek against his chest. "Well, I don't think you can chase away my hunger while I sleep. We should get dressed and check on Aris, too. I want to see how he's feeling."

Elios kissed her again, his skilled tongue teasing her until her body craved more, making the thoughts of leaving their room flee her mind, at least for a while. When he pulled away, she yanked him back to her, pouring every ounce of passion she could into the next kiss, her earlier hunger replaced with hunger of a different sort.

Snaking his arms around her, Elios rolled onto his back, pulling her on top of him. Her center lined up perfectly with his hard length as she straddled him, setting her body aflame, and suddenly she wished she had gone to sleep naked like he did last night. Her hips rolled of their own accord, dragging his shaft along the apex of her thighs, the cloth between them maddening. Even with her trousers, the sensation was delicious, eliciting a moan from her as her back arched with the pleasure of his hardness sliding against her clit.

Elios took advantage of her exposed neck, leaning up to suck the sensitive flesh into his mouth as he rocked his hips to meet hers. He would mark her flesh with the attention he was giving her neck, but she didn't care. It was too hot, her tunic too thick against the warmth of his bare skin. Rising onto her knees, Azure untied her top and threw it to the side of the bed. His wicked grin was the only warning she received before Elios rolled them again.

"Hey!" Her protest was cut short as he ripped her trousers off, tearing the fabric from her body.

Sliding his hand between their bodies, Elios grasped his cock, using the already glistening tip to trace her folds in teasing circles. She groaned, a combination of frustration and pleasure, as he slid his hardness from her clit to her entrance, dipping in only slightly and coating himself in her arousal.

Before she could complain about her need to have him inside her, Elios slammed into her all the way to the hilt. With the legs thrown up, her groans turned into moaning gasps and screams as he pounded into her, his thrusts punishing. Thoughts were impossible to form as each rough stroke brought her higher, making her belly coil tighter and tighter, ready to fracture.

"Fuck. Azure. You feel so damn good."

She was so close. *So close.* "Please. Elios." Her plea was nothing more than a breath as she begged for release.

Letting out a guttural groan, Elios' mouth went to her neck, biting to the brink of pain and then sucking the edge away. Azure's climax blasted through her like a tidal wave, her teeth biting into the blanket as she tried to quiet her screams, but when her climax launched into his, those final deep thrusts sent his name shouting from her lips.

Her head was too dazed, and her body too sated, for her to care. Their need for each other wouldn't allow them to take things slow, and that kind of intensity was impossible to handle in silence.

Azure and Elios went downstairs after they had bathed and dressed, finding their uninjured companions already drinking coffee in the tavern. It was a rustic and charming space, covered in wood planking, just like the rest of the building. Exposed hardwood beams supported the upper floor, and the far wall was lined with several windows. They were as small as the ones in the guestrooms, keeping the tavern dimly lit.

The wooden door that served as the establishment's entrance was covered in locks and boards to reinforce it when it was bolted shut. The locking mechanisms seemed like overkill, but after seeing a vampire up close, Azure didn't blame them for the added security.

Joining the others at their table, they thanked Georgios as he set two cups of coffee and plates of breakfast in front of them.

"How's Aris?" Elios asked as he took a bite of porridge.

Dimitris wiped his mouth with a napkin before responding. "He's in a lot of pain, so Phaedra has been administering a relief tonic often, which makes him tired. He's asleep now."

Hearing how much pain the man was in saddened Azure and sent her guilt rocketing to the forefront of her mind. She knew if it had not been for her, he wouldn't have gotten attacked. Nausea flipped her stomach, and she forced down a bite of food in the vain attempt to settle it. The eggs, porridge, and bread were flavorful, even if she was slightly queasy.

Elios dug into his breakfast as though he hadn't eaten in a week. "Anyone send a message to Kimon?"

Markos nodded. "This morning. Told him we're here and received a response a short while ago. The safe house will be ready for us tomorrow. I'm not sure if Aris will be ready to move yet, though. One of us may need to stay behind with him. I hate to leave his care to Georgios and Phaedra while he's so injured. Phaedra can care for him, but he's too big for her to lift on her own."

Dimitris nodded as he lifted his coffee mug, taking a sip before speaking. "I'll stay with him if need be. You two should get these ladies to the house when it's ready. They'll be more comfortable there. And safer."

Elios raised his mug in Dimitris' direction like he was making a toast. "Thank you for offering, Brother. But I can't help but wonder if you're only willing to stay behind to sample the drinks in this fine establishment."

Azure and Ocevia giggled, and even Markos' face spread into a wide grin. Dimitris' drunken night around the Arcane tribe's fire was not something they would let him forget anytime soon.

"Those drinks won't be on the house either," Georgios called out from behind the bar. "I'll have your ass washing dishes."

Their red-haired companion balled up his napkin and tossed it at Elios, nearly making it onto his plate. "Ha. Ha. Funny, really." Dimitris looked over his shoulder toward the bar. "Not you, Old Man. I'll wash dishes if you need help. It's better than washing Aris' ass." Smirking, he returned to look at them. "Anyway, what's on the agenda for today, boss?" His question was aimed at Elios, and Azure was surprised to realize there was a pecking order among their ranks. Pushing his empty plate away, Elios leaned back in his chair, wrapping his arm around her shoulders.

"I would say to remain hidden, but we need ears on the ground in case Miris' people show up asking questions. I don't want to be blindsided."

The sound of the Sea Goddess' name made Azure shudder. No matter how hard she tried to forget she was on the run, she couldn't escape reality.

Markos stood, leaning over to kiss Ocevia on the lips. The mermaid looked positively in love, and Azure understood the feeling. "I'll go speak with Phaedra about reaching out to our contacts in the city. I'll be back soon."

Ocevia watched her lover walk away, a silly smile on her face. Azure thought her friend might chase after him, but she didn't. She gently squeezed Elios' thigh before moving to the seat Markos vacated, and Ocevia looked relieved as she sat down.

With everything going on over their travels, as well as the men who held their attention, the two had little time to talk.

"Well..." Azure dragged out the word, her teasing tone filling her friend's porcelain cheeks with a brilliant blush.

"Well, what?" She knew Ocevia understood what she was getting at, but the blond chose to play coy, anyway.

Azure waggled her eyebrows. "Tell me how all of *that* happened." She motioned her hand between Ocevia, and the direction Markos disappeared in. "No judgment, of course. Elios and I got together fast as well. I'm just curious."

Her friend glanced at the men at the table, clearly the reason she was acting so shy, and then leaned in closer to Azure. Ocevia was not usually a bashful person but being around a group of men seemed to change that. She was quieter, more reserved, once the others joined them in Starspell. "From the moment I saw him standing outside the tavern, I knew he was mine. I couldn't deny my interest in him. I wanted the chance to see what we could be."

Azure knew that feeling all too well. Her connection to Elios had been undeniable from the start. "I felt the same way when I saw Elios clinging to those rocks after the shipwreck. Out of everyone that night..." Azure peeked at Elios and Dimitris to see if they were listening, but both men were engaged in conversation on the other side of the table while Georgios set up behind the bar. She lowered her voice, just in case. "Out of everyone who died that night, he fought so hard to survive. I couldn't take my eyes off him. It felt like a sign. Like I was meant to find him. I may have carried him to that island, but we saved each other."

Ocevia sipped her tea and took Azure's hand. "Do you think we can get away with this? I mean, *actually* get away with it. I can't help but feel like Miris' eyes are on us everywhere we go. I don't want to go back, Azure. I can't leave Markos."

Knowing the blond mermaid was just as worried as she was opened a pit in Azure's stomach. She wished there was a way to ensure they would escape the Sea Goddess. Instead, they were bystanders in their own fate, and she felt as helpless as she had on the day Daneliya drowned. She squeezed her friend's hand. "I would be lying if I said I wasn't worried. All I know is that these men will stop at nothing to keep us safe. We should find some comfort in that."

The side of Ocevia's mouth tipped up in a half smile, but it didn't reach her eyes. Their underlying fears may never fade away, no matter how long they evaded Miris' clutches. Elios and Dimitris stood, catching the women's attention and signaling the end of their conversation.

CHAPTER TWENTY-TWO
THIEVES IN THE NIGHT

Exploring Ceveasea was off limits. As much as Azure wanted to experience living among humans again, she understood the ban. The city was the largest populated area nearest Starspell, and it was likely Miris' people would search for the runaway mermaids there.

Even Elios stayed inside, not willing to risk discovery. There was little doubt in Azure's mind that the Sea Goddess knew of his existence, of the soul she had stolen from her. The only thing keeping him safe was that the evil deity did not know his identity, but if Lucia or Oona survived, that minimal protection was gone.

Markos and Dimitris were the only ones who left the inn to gather supplies and covertly meet with their contacts, searching for signs of the ones hunting them.

Ocevia and Azure spent their morning helping Phaedra around the building and caring for Aris. The latter slept most of the day, only requiring help to reposition himself and to administer pain tonic. Even though he had only been injured the night before, he seemed to be improving quickly under the healer's care. This brought Azure a smidgen of relief.

As the tavern's opening time approached, Azure and Elios went to the kitchens to help Georgios prepare dinner. Azure knew very little about cooking, aside from the basic meals she used to make for Daneliya, so she stuck to washing dishes and cutting vegetables.

The busy work kept her mind off Miris. Georgios was a chatty man who loved to reminisce about the past. He and Elios had many stories between them, some dangerous, but each one was as full of adventure as the last. The older man had apparently been very active in The Circle's activities before he found his wife and settled down in the border city. Azure laughed nearly the entire time, and it was a breath of fresh air after all the stress of recent days.

Unlike when they had arrived, people poured into the building as soon as they'd unlatched the door. The late afternoon sun streamed inside as the front door continued to open like it was the most popular place in the city. Azure, Ocevia, and Elios wore their hooded capes to hide their faces from the patrons, just in case Miris' people happened upon the establishment. The trio sat in a booth in a dark corner, talking amongst themselves for a few hours, not wanting to be confined in their chambers, but trying to avoid notice.

Both Markos and Dimitris mingled with the customers, listening to conversations, and sometimes joining in, hoping to catch wind of any sightings of the Sea Goddess' underlings. The two men had spent most of the day out in town for the same reason, and from what they gathered, their group were the only new arrivals. If Miris' people were in the town, they were hiding it well.

Unlike most taverns, where people partied until all hours of the night, the crowd of The Dusty Lantern thinned out as the sun started to sink behind the buildings. Once the last of its patrons left for the night, their group helped to clean up. With the hospitality shown to them by Georgios and Phaedra, it was the least they could do.

Azure was surprised when a familiar face entered the main room as she washed dishes behind the bar. Aris, sitting in some sort of rolling wooden chair, grinned from ear to ear. Everyone stopped what they were doing and approached him, excited to see him up and about.

Elios cupped his friend on the shoulder. "How are you feeling, brother?"

Sighing, Aris rubbed along his leg. "Pretty good, considering. My leg and ribs hurt like hell, but I'm glad to have this rolling chair." Propelling the wheels with his hands, Aris moved forward a few inches and then back again. "Phaedra had Georgios bring it in from storage. I can't get up the stairs, but at least I can make it to the bathroom by myself. Having someone help me piss does little for my warrior image."

A slow smile spread across Azure's lips as she watched Aris chat with the group. She had been really worried about him, guilt hovering like a dark cloud, so it was a relief to see him getting around on his own and in good spirits. He couldn't walk on his own yet, but he was certainly on his way to recovery. The best part was that he didn't seem to hold any animosity against her or Ocevia for getting injured while protecting them. Her group was still talking with Aris as she kissed Elios on the cheek and headed for the bathroom.

The corridor separating the tavern and infirmary was dark, just as it was the night before, a single lantern responsible for illuminating the entire space. The lone flame cast a faint glow, creating eerie shadows that made her blood chill. Azure was alone, giving the hall a more sinister feeling. She didn't know where Phaedra was, but the infirmary was empty.

Taking the lantern from the table outside the bathroom and lighting it, Azure brought it into the dark room with her. After relieving her bladder, she splashed cold water on her face while gazing into the looking glass that hung on the wall.

Her stomach dropped as an overwhelming sense of fear washed over her, prickling her skin, but she didn't know why. Aris was getting better, and none of Miris' people had come to the tavern asking for them, but the ominous feeling still plagued her, making her senses too alert, her sweat feeling icy against her skin.

When she opened the door to leave the bathroom, her entire body froze. Heart going into overdrive, terror made it impossible to pass through the open frame, like the universe itself was warning her of danger.

Taking a deep breath to steal her frayed nerves, Azure ignored the innate warning. Once she rejoined the others, she would feel better. She always felt safer when she was by Elios' side. Grabbing the lantern, she took a step into the hallway.

A single step. That was as far as she got before a clammy hand slapped against her mouth, gripping her face painfully tight while another arm had an ironclad hold on her waist. She tried to scream and flail, anything to get free and alert her friends that she was in trouble, but the hand pressed tighter, muffling her frantic cries, as something pinched and burned inside her neck. The last thing she remembered was the sound of the lantern's glass shattering as it hit the floor before blackness consumed her.

Consciousness sporadically teased Azure, brief flashes that made no sense. An ice body at her back. Her hands bound in front of her. Hooves thundering at a gallop over rocky terrain.

She didn't see her captor, nor did she recognize their voice, not that they spoke to her. The movement of the horse pulled her under again, her mind too hazy to understand what was happening and her body too weak to fight.

Flames flickered, pulling Azure back from induced unconsciousness. The rope binding her wrists, now secured behind her back, was fastened so tight her fingers were numb. She tried to scream but couldn't. A dirty cloth that tasted of dust and sweat was stuffed between her teeth, gagging her. Her surroundings blurred in and out as her head spun, and when the view came into focus, she wished it hadn't.

The mountain pass filled her vision, and a fresh wave of terror hit her. This was the last place she wanted to be now that the night ruled. The evil-filled crimson slits of the decapitated vampire's eyes flashed through her mind. It was too dangerous to be here. She struggled against her ties, but it was no use. They were too tight. The fight drained out of her along with her energy and her shoulders slumped.

"Don't bother, Azure. You won't be getting away again." The voice, so full of hatred, was familiar. Her addled brain struggled to place it, but she didn't have to ponder for long. Torch in hand, her attacker stepped out from the shadows, the last face she wanted to see illuminated in the firelight.

Matted blond hair framed an expression full of malice. *Lucia.* She was alive. Azure looked around frantically, but Oona was nowhere to be seen. *Did the Kraken kill Oona, or did the duo separate to hunt her? Was Lucia alone, or would the magic-wielding mermaid join them soon?* The only relief she felt was that Elios and Ocevia weren't there with her. She fervently hoped they would notice she had been taken, and her loved ones would move somewhere safe.

"Let me go." Azure's desperate command was garbled by the gag as she struggled against her bindings again, but there was no loosening the ties. All she was doing was wearing herself out.

Lucia watched; amusement clear on her feral face. The mermaid showed no fear of her captive, nor of the vampires that hunted within the mountains. Lucia was far too unhinged to feel afraid. Azure tried to break free again, kicking her legs in a useless attempt to increase her strength.

Lucia's smile was vicious, madness swirling in the turquoise depths of her eyes. "This is for Oona, you stupid bitch." The mermaid's fist collided with Azure's temple, and unconsciousness claimed her once more.

Her legs screamed in pain as she was dragged along the ground, broken stones biting into her flesh. Yanked into the sea without warning, Azure choked on the water as it filled her lungs. Using the last of her energy, she shifted into her mermaid form and breathed fully, her lungs easing their burning protest.

Whatever Lucia had used to drug her still flowed through her veins, blurring the edges of reality. Her captor paid her no mind, not giving her the chance to swim along. Azure's tail dragged along the bottom of the sea, coral and rocks ripping chunks of her scales off. Each iridescent scale that was scraped off felt like a nail being torn from its root. She cried out; the sound garbled below the water. The pain was excruciating, but it was nothing compared to the fate that awaited her. Their destination was clear, and Azure knew she would not survive.

CHAPTER TWENTY-THREE
I OWN YOU

Miris' underwater lair came into view after hours of being dragged along the sea floor. Azure's battered tail throbbed in agony, but every time unconsciousness gave her a bit of relief, Lucia would yank on the chains that bound her wrists to wake her, the cold metal biting deeper into her torn flesh. She didn't know when the rope bindings were replaced, but the skin that had been rubbed raw when she tried to break free was now openly bleeding from the wounds.

She clenched her jaw as she swallowed her cries, not wanting to give the insane merbitch the satisfaction. Her pulse raced with the need to run, to fight, but she couldn't. She was bound, injured, and weak, and she was being led into a compound filled with beings whose sole purpose in life was to kill.

The metal gate surrounding the Goddess' illusive palace opened, and Lucia yanked her past the countless mermaids and mermen who filled the grounds, all staring at her. Their expressions ranged from surprised and frightened, to malicious and bloodthirsty, but no one intervened as Lucia shoved Azure into the airlock that separated the watery courtyard from the splendor within.

The power in the space forced her damaged tail to shift, leaving her naked, and her legs were just as shredded. Chunks of flesh were missing, while others barely hung on by a thread. The airlock dried their bodies, and Azure's stomach flipped dangerously as she watched the dangling bits of her skin sway in the hot wind. The pain grew so intense that it numbed her, like her mind left her body in order to preserve her sanity.

Miris' lair was far below the sea, but the Sea Goddess liked the finer things in life, those only found in the human lands. Her greed and need for extravagance outweighed her hatred for those that dwelled on land, and she filled the heart of her domain with only the best of the best.

Azure had only been inside a few times, but it was always to receive punishment for angering Miris, not to enjoy the palace's amenities. She tried to stumble to her feet before her captor began walking again, but her battered body was too slow. Lucia dragged her out of the airlock and through the gilded halls, leaving a trail of blood streaking along the marble floors.

All the open beauty of the palace faded, giving way to cold stone walls and uneven ground, as Azure was pulled through a nondescript door, barely managing to climb to her feet as Lucia tugged her metal leash.

The underwater castle was a lot like the goddess who ruled from it. Stunning on the outside, but cold and dark once you looked deeper. Azure hardly felt the damage the rough stone did to her bare feet as she went down a dark corridor behind Lucia. She didn't know where she was being taken, but she could guess.

For as many lashings as she'd received, Azure had never visited the palace's depths, but as the hall sloped downward, she became certain of their destination. Bile coated her throat, and she tried her best to swallow it. Fear would get her nowhere. Her only hope was to bide her time. She would die here, of that she had no doubt, but if she waited until the moment was right, she may be able to goad the sadistic merbitch, or the goddess, into killing her quickly. Elios' face swam into her mind, his words as he told her to survive resurfacing, but she shoved them down, afraid even thinking of him would somehow alert Miris of his identity.

Even with the protection of the airlock, the corridor was humid, the floor slippery and difficult to walk on. Azure slipped, her injured legs feeble beneath her, but Lucia didn't allow time for her to find her footing, yanking her chains impatiently and pressing on with no hesitation.

The drug she'd been given was beginning to wear off, and the deafening beat of her heart sent adrenaline buzzing through her. They walked down a maze of halls, each as dark as the last.

It was nearly impossible to keep track of the twists and turns, the corridors appearing identical.

Azure knew this was where Lucia was bringing her, but when she saw the dungeon, she couldn't stop the tremors that ran through her body. That torture chamber was every mermaid's greatest fear. No one ever came back alive.

A beast of a guard stood sentinel outside the entrance, wearing no more than a tight pair of pants and boots. His exposed torso was covered in bulky muscles and littered with scars, making him massively intimidating. His hair was dark brown and wavy, falling below his shoulders. Deep brown eyes, a heavy brow, and a jagged scar across his face convinced her he was good at his job, whatever that may be. To receive such brutal injuries and survive? The man was someone to fear, but he didn't seem interested in joining whatever hell she was about to endure. He merely grunted and dipped his head, stepping aside to let them in.

Lucia slammed the heavy metal door behind them and dragged Azure over to the far wall, locking heavy shackles around her ankles. The restraints, bolted to the rock wall, were lined with sharp metal spikes that pierced her skin, a painful reminder she wasn't going anywhere. Struggling was futile, and even if she tried, the spikes would drive further into her. Her limbs felt too heavy, and the backs of her eyes burned, but she held back her tears. She would be strong and endure until she was granted her last breath.

After she was secured, Lucia's lips curled as she let out an animalistic snarl, looking as feral as she did when she circled Elios on the beach. Azure didn't even have time to tense before Lucia's fist slammed into her stomach. She doubled over in pain, gasping as Lucia's fist collided with the side of her face. Her cheekbone screamed as she collapsed on the ground, the taste of blood coating her tongue.

A sob tore from her, a sob she'd held back since she was taken from the tavern, and it made her angry with herself. She couldn't protect herself, always relying on Elios and The Circle, and now she couldn't even contain her cries. She felt weak, pitiful. Lucia said nothing as she stared down at Azure's crumbled form, a look of triumph and malicious delight twisting her face as she pulled the gag from Azure's mouth and stormed out of the cell, the heavy door slamming behind her.

Azure remained on the cold stone floor as time slipped past, panting as she held her throbbing face. She was starving and exhausted, hopelessness poisoning her heart as her mind kept circling back to her friends. Ocevia and Elios were wanted by Miris too, so why was she the only one who was captured? She was thankful the others were safe, but what if Miris sent another mermaid to abduct them, too?

The thought made her chest cave, making breathing impossible. She hoped with every fiber of her being that she was the only one to be captured. She wanted her friends to continue evading Miris' people, to finally be free, even if she never saw them again. Agony pulsated through her entire body, and she knew the injuries would keep being dealt, but nothing hurt as much as her heart. She needed Elios and Ocevia to survive, to escape Miris.

Please be okay.

Metal scraping on metal tore Azure from the relief of unconsciousness. She rubbed her eyes, not remembering where she was, and jolted as her vision adjusted to the dank cell, her mutilated legs screaming in pain as she moved. A lantern flickered near the door, casting a weak light around the room. She was the only one in there, thankfully, but a tray laid on the floor, holding a pitiful ration of water and dried fish. She groaned, not knowing if her stomach would be able to handle any food, let alone that disgusting excuse for a meal. Still, it was better to try than to starve, so she bit down on the paper-thin flesh, nearly gagging as the flavor hit her tongue.

The dungeon was windowless. There was no need with only the darkened sea outside, but the total isolation battered one's sanity and made time obsolete.

The small lantern was the only source of light, but there wasn't much to see. Four stone walls, about six feet wide, formed her cell. There was a contraption in the corner to relieve herself in, and a small sink and faucet. A thin cloth blanket was sprawled out on the dirty floor to serve as a bed, and the only decoration was the metal bolts drilled into the rock face, securing her shackles.

Voices on the other side of the door grew closer, stealing her attention from the dank surroundings. She held her breath and listened, but the metal muffled the sound too much to make out the words. A lock clicked, a heavy bolt screeched, and the metal door swung open with a high-pitched squeal. The light from the corridor streamed into the shadowed cell, highlighting her visitor's form.

Miris.

The Sea Goddess stepped into the dingy dungeon, flanked by two giant male guards. Azure retreated as far from the door as she could and stumbled to her feet, her heart beating dangerously fast. She hadn't expected to see Miris show up in her cell. Summon her to the great hall to torture her? Sure. She had done that plenty of times before. Send one of her underlings to torture her? Likely. But show herself in a damp, musty dungeon? She was the sort to only surround herself in luxury, and her appearance in such a grim environment showed how angry she was with her prisoner.

The Sea Goddess stared at Azure, expression frighteningly blank, as she motioned for the men to leave.

One of the guards looked alarmed, and the other shook his head, trying to object. "Your..."

Miris cut him off before he could finish his thought. "Don't you dare question me. Get. Out." Her face contorted, rage that boiled under the surface leaking out, as she spoke in a commanding tone, leaving no opening for argument. The guards bowed at the waist and left without another word, shutting the door. Azure clenched her fists at her sides to hide their trembling.

Eyes the color of quicksilver narrowed in on her, making the hair on the back of her neck stand up. The Sea Goddess was beautiful on the outside, but she was evil personified. She was tall and slender, with thick onyx hair that fell in perfect silky waves to her waist and draped over her breasts, framing her high cheekbones and full lips. Sheer fire-red material wrapped around her arms and torso, with thicker patches of lace over her breasts and groin. The outfit covered much, yet hid very little, but it was her stare that held Azure immobile. The silver irises swirled like a whirlpool and were framed by thick, impossibly dark lashes, her liquid metal eyes both mesmerizing and unsettling.

"You stole from me, Azure." Miris paused, twirling the golden necklace that fell between her breasts. The diamond nautilus sparkled as it caught the faint light of the lantern. Azure didn't dare argue. It wouldn't change anything. She was at Miris' mercy. "The male you stole, his soul belongs to me." The Sea Goddess' face split into a horrifying grin, showcasing the evil within. Azure failed to stifle a shudder as the full force of Miris' eyes focused on her, the silver shining with greed and cruelty. "And I will get him back."

"Please." A sob broke free at the thought of Elios standing defenseless beneath that vicious stare broke her. "You can do anything you want to me. Just please let him go."

Miris let out a sadistic cackle as she waved Azure's plea away like she was swatting an insect. "Oh, darling. You're quite amusing sometimes. I will do what I want with you, but you are mistaken if you believe you hold any say here. I do not need your permission, little mermaid. I own you. I own your soul. A flick of my wrist and your bloody legs will shift into a tail. Another flick and that tail will rot away, slowly eating you alive, until the rot finally reaches your pathetic chest and stops your heart." Her grin spread wider, like she'd just told a hilarious joke. "But, of course, I won't do that, darling. You disobeyed me, and you *will* be punished, but I would never let you die that easily. First, I'll retrieve my stolen property, and then I'll make you watch as I devour his soul."

"No. Please." Azure dropped to her knees, lowering her forehead to the stones in supplication. The urge to fight, to flee, surged through her, but she was chained to the wall, and anything she did to upset the evil goddess could be taken out on Elios. "Please let him go."

Miris threw her head back and laughed, crossing the floor in two giant strides. Azure barely managed not to flinch as the lanky shadow darted at her. The goddess gripped Azure by the hair and yanked her up onto her knees, pulling back until she was forced to stare into the silver swirls of insanity.

"Oh, naïve little darling. Did you fall in love with the boy? Did his soul call to you?"

Miris let go of her hair and gripped her face roughly, her injured cheekbone exploding at the intense pressure. "Did you share your body with him, little mermaid? Is that why you're so attached to what is mine? Don't worry. You may have forged a life bond with him when you saved him, but I'll spare your heart and sever that connection. I'll ride his cock while you watch and show you how one truly pleases a man. If you're lucky, maybe your *love* will fade before I make you watch me swallow his soul."

The deranged goddess tightened her grip on Azure's face, her nails digging into flesh, before she threw the injured mermaid away from her. Azure collided with the wall, the back of her skull cracking against the stone, but that didn't hurt as much as her chest. Fear for Elios consumed her. She didn't care what was done to her, but if Miris did the things she promised... She couldn't finish the thought. She silently prayed that Elios and Ocevia fled the city and went deeper into hiding.

"My riders are already on their way to Ceveasea. They will find him, and when they do, I'll be back to do what I promised. Hope you're ready for the show, little mermaid."

Chapter Twenty-Four
MIRIS' THREATS

Warmth from the bonfire's flames licked at Azure's skin, bathing the dark cave in a romantic glow. Shivers chased the calloused fingers that trailed along the shape of her curves, sensual and thorough caresses that made her toes curl.

Her eyes closed as she enjoyed the moment of pure bliss. She could stay there forever. Elios' scent filled her nose as his warm lips traced up the column of her neck, making her come alive with burning desire. There was nothing in the world she craved the way she did him. Sucking in a breath, she pulled his face to hers and kissed him, pouring every ounce of need she felt into it. Elios groaned and wrapped his arms around her, pressing his forehead to hers as his cerulean eyes stared into her very soul.

"I love you." His words touched deep inside her, healing her fragmented heart piece by piece. She knew he meant it, and the fact that she thought she would never be loved made the sentiment all the sweeter.

"I love you, too."

T he cell door swung open, the hinges squealing, as the door banged against the stone wall. Azure shot up, tears filling her eyes as she woke. The dream with Elios had been so vivid, so real, and it hit her like reality with a cold, cruel bucket of water. Loud footsteps thudded toward her, but the solitary lantern was as dim as her hope, and she couldn't see who thundered at her.

The person hauled her to her feet, and she fought back on instinct. Body flailing, she tried to get free, but shackled feet hindered her. She flew up into the air and dangled there, a giant arm encircling her waist.

"Don't try to fight it, little fish." The voice was deep and gruff, and she didn't recognize it. The man set her on her feet and wrapped a hand around her forearm before releasing the shackles that secured her to the wall. Craning her neck, she tried to see who held her. She couldn't see his face, but he smelled of rusted metal and unwashed bodies. Azure made one feebler attempt to rip herself from his grasp, but his ironclad hold didn't loosen. "You're coming with us."

Another large man waited just outside the cell door, covered by a hooded cloak that left only his lips visible. The sight of him made her blood chill.

The two men were silent as they led her deeper into the dungeon. Every step down the winding halls felt like she was walking closer to her doom. Her escorts moved swiftly, making it impossible for her to make a mental map of the layout, and they gave nothing away about their destination.

She twisted, trying to see the face of the man who dragged her along, but he was too tall, and the lighting too dim. All she could see was a dark, heavily tattooed arm that was thicker than her thigh. She clenched her jaw, trying to appear brave as she forced back the tears that begged to fall. She refused to cry again, at least not when they could see her.

Their steps slowed as they reached a fork in the hallway. Turning left, the men pulled her through an open doorway. The room was larger than her cell and just as poorly lit. Humidity made the air thick, saltwater and mildew overpowering her nose. The stone walls and floor were slick and coated with condensation, and dripping water echoed around the space as though the sea were preparing to reclaim its territory. Chains hung from the ceiling like an ominous chandelier waiting for its centerpiece. Azure squeezed her eyes shut as her lips trembled, trying, but failing, to calm herself.

The man dragged her forward, switching her hold to her wrists. Pulling her arms straight up, he trapped her with the dangling manacles. He left her hanging there, naked and exposed, and stood in the corner, leaning against the wall. She swayed in place, her shoulders already aching from the pressure of her weight and struggled to gain her footing to ease the burden on her joints, but her pointed toes barely skimmed the ground. She didn't bother pleading with her captors. As terrifying as her life was now, this was something she was familiar with, at least.

Lashings were Miris' favorite punishment. Her vanity showed in the way she tormented the mermaids who displeased her. No doubt the beautiful goddess would rather die than have her skin marred, but it didn't bother Azure. The pain was excruciating, but temporary. It would fade, leaving behind more scars to tell the story of how many times she'd angered the Sea Goddess.

The man in the hooded cloak did not speak as he approached, reaching for the leather whip hanging on the wall. Her body trembled, muscle memory creating phantom pains as she watched him step toward her.

He lifted his head, the hood sliding back enough to show his face, which was covered with a leather mask that had crude openings cut out for his eyes and mouth. His twisted smile showed through the gaping hole, teeth gleaming viciously as he snapped the whip, the teasing crack in the air making her flinch. He looked like a monster, and the excitement in his dark eyes made her stomach heave. She yanked at her manacles, unsuccessfully trying to pull herself free, but he didn't react, only continued to prowl toward her like a predator, ready to pounce.

The whip cracked again, but this one wasn't a taunt. Fire spread across the front of her thighs, blood oozing out from the broken flesh. Her body jerked, trying to curl in on itself, but the manacles held her position firm. Teeth clenched, she took shallow breaths, but he didn't give her time to prepare herself before the next lash split her stomach.

His sadistic laughter, the snap of the whip, and her screams were the only sounds that filled the room.

Crack. Crack. Crack. Crack. Crack.

She couldn't even tell where he'd hit first. The rapid succession of the strikes made it impossible to know where one ended and the next began. All she knew was that her entire body felt like it was doused in fuel and set aflame. The burning pain was too much. All her lashings to date were concentrated on her back, but this time was different. The man prowled around her hanging form, scanning her body for unmarred flesh to break.

Another snap of the whip and Azure screamed, losing her precarious footing as her body swung with the force of the strikes, the cuffs tearing at her already raw wrists.

He continued to circle her, looking for another fresh place to strike. *Another and another.* There was never any warning. Sometimes the lashes were spaced out, and other times they struck in quick succession. She lost track of how many times the whip carved into her skin. Her head hung, the agony threatening to pull her under. Spots danced in her vision, and she willed her body to give up.

Burning pain flared on her back as she swayed with her eyes closed, jolting them back open. He took aim at her healed scars, reveling at his skill when he managed to reopen perfectly. It was hard, her abuser explained, to strike the same exact spot twice.

"It's easier, you know, if you're the one who dealt the original blow, but I haven't had the pleasure of decorating your body before. If I aim for my own mark, I bet I could hit it exactly right, nine out of ten times. Should we test it? Yes. I think so."

Azure didn't respond to him, or his taunts. She just set her jaw as he carved into her flesh, his strike landing in the same location over and over. Did he hit the same spot nine out of ten times? Thankfully, she didn't know. The torture was too much, and her body went limp, unconscious, unable to function under the agony any longer.

The raging fire of her wounds faded some, thanks to her mermaid healing. She didn't know how long she had been unconscious for, but her lashes were no longer open, so it must have been for quite a while. Her skin was littered with angry red welts that would scar, adding to those she already had, like a roadmap of her pain.

The lashings were always like that. The marks would heal like every other injury, but there was something special about the whips they used. Any other wound healed without a trace, but the whip marks never disappeared. She looked at the massive raised lines on her thighs, belly, and breasts. Would Elios be disgusted at the sight of her now? Not that it mattered. She hoped she never saw him again, because if she did, that meant Miris got her claws in him. The goddess' threat echoed in her mind.

I'll ride his cock while you watch and show you how one truly pleases a man.

Azure screamed in frustration, grabbing the food tray someone left beside her and slinging it at the wall. The water splattered, dried fish shooting in all directions, and the metal platter clattered to the floor loudly. It wasn't enough to release her anger, her terror. Everything was too much. She wanted to rage and destroy. She wanted to cry. She wanted to scream. Something, anything, to release the overwhelming emotions that were drowning her in that underwater cell.

She wished the sea would level Miris' lair and wash away all the evil that took place there, wash her completely away. She was done, so done. What was the point anymore? Why did fate lead Elios to her, only to let them suffer a crueler future? Death would be a welcome respite from the hell she had lived in her short life. The freedom of fading away called to her. If she bit her tongue off, she could probably bleed to death before the guard noticed. If she made the spikes of the shackles dig in deeper, that would speed up the process. Her plan started to take form, but then Elios' blue eyes and loving smile filled her mind, his expression when he asked her to live. She couldn't give up, not yet. If she had to endure the torment for the rest of her life, it would be worth it just to know if he evaded Miris. He was her life-mate, and she loved him. He was everything in a world where she had nothing else. She didn't believe in ghosts, or the afterlife, but if such things existed, she knew her spirit would never rest if she didn't know his fate.

Chapter Twenty-Five
Purpose in Life

Time passed with no more visits from the Sea Goddess. How much? Azure couldn't be sure. Every day was the same, or maybe she'd spent some time unconscious in between. There was no way to tell. The only way to mark how long she had been in the cell was to count the torture sessions, and even that was uncertain. Did he beat her daily? Every other day? Multiple times in one?

All she knew was it felt like it was often. Too often. The hooded man took her back to that same room, shackled her arms above her head, and attacked her. Sometimes, his whip bit into her. Other times, his knife carved out chunks of her flesh and muscle. It was fun for him, *a game*. He liked to see which injuries took longer for her body to heal. The whip marks continued to leave an abstract painting of scars over her body, but the knife wounds always vanished. Azure thought it must have hurt his pride when the wounds healed well, because the torture sessions were always worse when she came back in one piece.

When the intensity of the attacks grew worse, at least she passed out faster. Her abuser toyed with the idea of seeing how fast her bones would take to heal, but he decided against it. He didn't want his toy damaged for too long.

Time continued to pass as she went through the motions. She shifted and wet her tail from the small sink on most days, but she still didn't even know if it was truly necessary, or if it was just a lie told by the Sea Goddess to torment her. Most days tested her resolve to live. Still, she was determined to survive, if only to see Elios never arrive in the dungeon. Every endless moment that passed was filled with that little comfort. Life was barely worth living, and her entire body wanted nothing more than to quit existing, but at least Miris hadn't found him yet.

The meals slipped through the slot at the bottom of the door were unsubstantial. Weight fell off her already slim figure, and unlike the knife wounds, it didn't come back. Her ribs had begun to jut through her skin, and her stomach was always grumbling. It was a pathetic existence.

Periods of numbness, alternating with stints of feeling too much, filled her solitary moments. When the leather masked monster wasn't torturing her, she saw Elios, Ocevia, and Daneliya in her dreams, sometimes even in her waking moments. After a particularly vicious torture session, her fractured mind conjured up a realistic vision of her lover. He held her, comforted her, and said he loved her, but when her wounds healed, and the fog cleared, the illusion broke, leaving her empty.

The dreams were pleasant, but waking was always heartbreaking. They were always there to give her love and support, to tell her to stay strong, but when her eyes opened, she was alone. She tried to numb her emotions, tried to harden her heart like she used to, but it was impossible. There were too many people she loved and worried about now, and she couldn't suppress those feelings. *Harden her heart.* It wasn't an easy part to play, but she kept working at it.

She laid on the cold floor, freezing under the sorry excuse of a blanket, counting the stones on the wall. Anything to pass the dull waking moments. If only she could sleep forever.

She was on ninety-seven when she heard the telltale sign of the squeaky hinges. She snapped her eyes shut, pretending to be unconscious. Her flesh was still littered with open wounds. Another beating might actually be the death of her. How much could her body take before it shut down for good? Not daring to move, she tried to keep her breathing level as she prayed the men believed her ruse.

The gentle touch of a cool rag startled her out of her act, and she sat up as fast as she could, scrambling backward until she was pressed into the corner.

A red-haired female stared at her, rag still in hand, hovering over where Azure's body just was. She knew the woman was a mermaid by her turquoise eyes. They all had the exact same eye color, a mark of their cursed servitude. Appearing no older than Azure, with porcelain skin and a splash of freckles, the mermaid held her hands up and stepped forward slowly, like she was approaching a wounded animal.

"I didn't mean to frighten you. I thought you were unconscious still. My name is Corileia. I was sent to clean your wounds, but I didn't want to wake you."

"Why now? I've been here for... I don't even know how long." It wasn't that she didn't believe the female, but it didn't make sense. Why bother tending to her now, after countless beatings?

"For a week. I've been cleaning your injuries every day. Haven't you wondered how you've been healing so fast? I've been applying a balm to enhance your healing while you sleep."

Azure wasn't sure if she should thank Corileia or hit her. It had been nice to wake up without gaping wounds. However, the faster she healed, the sooner she was brutalized again.

"A week? Only a week? It felt like an eternity."

Corileia grimaced, and Azure shared her name awkwardly. It wasn't as if she was going to say, "nice to meet you." It wasn't nice to meet *anyone* while in Miris' dungeons.

"I know who you are. And yes, your condition has been quite bad."

Azure snorted at the understatement but held still as the red-haired female approached and began dabbing her wounds with the cool cloth again. She winced, sucking in a sharp breath through clenched teeth, as the disinfectant touched one of her open wounds, creating a fresh wave of anguish.

"Sorry. I'm sorry. I need to clean your wounds, so they don't get infected. You're in such a bad state, I'm not sure if your mermaid healing can handle it."

"It's okay." The words were broken by sharp gasps as she tried to breathe through the pain.

Although the disinfectant burned like scalding embers against her skin, Corileia's touch was gentle. "Tell me your story. Maybe focusing on something else will keep your mind off my ministrations."

Azure huffed a laugh. Nothing could get her mind off the excruciating wounds and the fiery burn of the cleaning solution. "What do you want to know?"

The mermaid poured more of the liquid onto the cloth, setting a glass bottle down beside her, and touched another gash, the fresh press of liquid fire making her jerk. "Sorry. Sorry." A cool hand touched Azure's shoulder in apology. She closed her eyes to the sensation. It felt like so long since anyone showed her comfort—showed her kindness.

"Is it true that you rescued a man from the sea and hid away with him?"

Her new acquaintance certainly knew how to distract her. "There don't seem to be any secrets around here."

Corileia chuckled. "None at all."

Azure was surprised Miris allowed such a rumor to spread, knowing it revealed a possible rebellion against her rule, but considering the state the runaway mermaid was in, it sent a message. It showed the others that they *could* rebel, but it would only be temporary. The Sea Goddess always won.

"It's true."

A soothing balm cooled the cleaned injuries, and she was grateful Corileia alternated between cleansing and soothing. "What made you decide to do something so bold? You had to know Miris would find out."

Azure clenched her teeth as the healer moved onto another wound but managed a simple shrug. "Something told me to save him. I couldn't sit there and watch him drown. It was like... my purpose in life, the reason I was cursed, was to save him."

Corileia leaned back on her heels, the open balm container forgotten in her hand. "Do you regret it?"

That was the easiest question Azure had ever been asked, and the resounding 'no' came easily from her lips. He was her life-mate. She didn't understand what that meant, hadn't been a mermaid long enough to know much of their ways, but she knew she had felt it from the moment she'd touched him. He was hers. At least until she was gone. Closing her eyes, she willed her burning eyes to stay dry.

The healer stared at her for a moment but didn't probe any further. She continued to purify and soothe the injuries in silence. A guard knocked a short time later, and Corileia was escorted from the room by her elbow, making it clear that she was not free within the palace, either. She may have been a healer, but she was a slave, nonetheless.

Azure returned to her fetal position on the floor, staring blankly at the stone. She wished she knew Corileia's story. The woman was kind, and it made Azure wonder why she'd made a bargain with Miris to begin with. They all had a story to tell.

The squeal of the metal door made Azure jump. She wasn't sure how long it'd been since the healer had left her cell. She didn't even know if she had fallen asleep, or just disassociated from herself all together, as she gazed at the unchanging stone.

Sitting up, she tried to prepare herself for another round of torture but came face-to-face with a new guard. This man was less intimidating, shorter and slimmer. His face was not covered by a hooded cloak either, to her relief.

"Where are you taking me?" she asked, watching him warily.

Crossing the room, the guard held out a set of manacles in front of her.

"The Sea Goddess requests your presence. Hands." He dipped his chin toward the waiting irons. Azure begrudgingly placed her wrists in the cuffs before he locked them snug around her.

"Miris wants me for what?" Her mind whirled. She wondered if her friends had been captured, or if perhaps the goddess had grown bored and it was finally the day she would be executed. She scanned his face, but he gave away nothing.

He pulled on her manacles to ensure they were secure and led her out of the cell. "I don't question my goddess, prisoner. I've been tasked with bringing you into the throne room. That is all."

She didn't want to go. At that moment, the dungeon felt like a safer place to be. But the chain running from her manacled wrists to his hand made the decision for her, and Azure followed the unnamed guard through the endless corridors and into the castle proper.

She had never been inside Miris' throne room, and she didn't know the way around the castle. Still, Azure scanned her surroundings as they walked, taking in every detail she could. If she ever got the chance to escape, she needed to have an escape route. The guards would be enough of a challenge without adding unfamiliar terrain into the equation. Not that she thought she would ever be able to escape, but it was a nice delusion to have.

After traipsing through countless rooms and halls, they arrived at a set of ornately carved double doors made of polished wood. A guard stood sentinel at the entrance, nodding to her escort and opening one door to admit them.

The throne room was every bit as stunning as the rest of the palace. Torches hung from one side of each of the six basalt columns, painting the hall in a brilliant range of yellows and oranges. The curved ceiling sported artistic depictions of sea creatures that danced in the flickering light while statues of mermaids looked down upon the mosaic floor of the imposing room. An ebony rug running up to the throne split to encircle the entire hall while rounded banners with embellished needlework draped from the walls. The banners, six in all, were lit on either side and illuminated the portraits of the fiercest creatures that lived in the underwater kingdom.

Miris sat in a large, intricately carved onyx throne, her long crimson gown spread across the stairs at her feet. The Sea Goddess' lips, painted in the same shade of red, were tipped up in a smirk as Azure was pulled before her. The look of satisfaction on the evil deity's face made her skin crawl and her heart drop simultaneously.

"Leave us." The guard did not hesitate. Bowing at the waist, he made a brisk exit, closing the door behind him. Everything in Azure wanted to look Miris in the eyes and mouth off, to enrage the goddess until she ended her for good. She barely refrained, aiming her eyes at the floor.

The sound of Miris' nails tapping rhythmically on the arm of her throne echoed through the large room. She was waiting for Azure to say something, but Azure wouldn't give her the pleasure.

Miris leaned forward on her throne. Azure could see her under lowered lashes as her smirk lifted into a cruel grin. "My scouts found your life-mate, and Ocevia. Pathetically weak excuse for a mermaid. She's more pathetic than even you."

Azure's heart stopped. Her head snapped up, and she looked at Miris before scanning the room. "Where are they?"

"They are still in Ceveasea, but they'll be here soon enough." Miris sighed loudly. "They're crafty, but they won't outrun me. I still have promises to keep to you, little mermaid."

Azure squeezed her eyes shut and ducked her head, hiding behind her hair to prevent Miris from seeing her terrified expression. Miris, appearing bored by Azure's lack of reaction, called for a guard to take her back to her cell.

CHAPTER TWENTY-SIX
RESCUE

A zure paced around the small cell, stretching her freshly healed skin. Her mind kept racing, the minimal activity doing nothing to drown her fears. If Miris got her hands on Elios and Ocevia, there was no telling what the Sea Goddess would order done to them while she was made to watch. She knew the goddess would kill her, kill all three of them, but death wouldn't come before they all lost their sanity.

A loud boom sounded from behind the metal door, followed by soft voices. She scurried back into the corner of her cell and waited, terrified. Sometimes, the hooded man would taunt her through the door before taking her to one of their *little sessions*, as he called them, but never did the noise from the corridor echo so fiercely.

A key scraped in the lock, and she broke out in a cold sweat as the bolt slid open. Her heart pounded so loud it muffled the creaky hinges as the door swung open. Her mouth went dry no matter how many times she tried to swallow, and she struggled to control her breathing, but it was no use. Each inhale was shallow, the air rushing in and out of her lungs too quickly, and her head began to spin.

A beautiful face, framed by long locks of blond hair, spilled through the door, and Azure was certain the end was near. She'd finally lost her mind. Blazing turquoise eyes bore into hers, and she was afraid to speak, afraid to shatter the illusion.

"Azure." Ocevia whispered, slipping into the cell. Another figure crept in behind her, leaving the door slightly ajar. The light of the lantern hit the woman's face, and she saw Corileia. Tears poured from Ocevia's eyes as she ran across the small room and hugged Azure so tight her exposed ribs groaned in protest. "I'm going to get you out of here."

Azure blinked rapidly, still not believing her eyes. She lifted a shaking hand, placing it on her friend's porcelain cheek. The damp streaks from her cries and the smoothness of the blond's skin convinced her this was real and not a figment of her fragmented mind. "You're really here. I don't understand. How did you get past the guards? Where's Elios? Everyone else? How did you join up with Corileia?"

Smiling, Ocevia wiped away her tears and nodded toward the doorway. "I hit that guard over the head with a metal lantern and knocked him out. I snuck past everyone else I came across, but there weren't many guards on the way here. I guess they figured you weren't a threat while you were chained up, but they weren't ready for me." Her best friend winked at her, but Azure could see the horror in her eyes as she stared at the new scars that marred Azure's exposed skin. Ocevia unlocked the shackles as she continued. "Everyone is fine. Dimitris stayed behind with Aris at the inn, and Elios and Markos are in boats above the palace, waiting for us to return. Corileia was in the cell next to yours. I opened it, looking for you, and she told me which one was yours. Figured she was worth saving since she cared about helping you."

Azure thanked the healer absentmindedly as her heart beat so fast, she could feel her pulse in her abdomen. Elios was so close, but she wasn't sure if her visceral reaction was from the prospect of seeing him or from the fear for his safety. He was too close to the crazed goddess. He wasn't safe. "Ocevia, we have to get Elios out of the sea. If Miris realizes he's here, she'll-" She trailed off, not brave enough to repeat the deity's threats aloud. "We have to get him far from the water."

Nodding, Ocevia reached for Azure's hand, pulling her to the door and peeking into the hallway. "No one's coming. Let's go. Corileia, do you know the way?"

The redhead nodded and led the way as the other two trailed behind, not daring to utter a word as they crept through the dark corridors.

The steep incline told them they were nearing the last door. Once they exited it, they would be inside the foyer. From there, they only had to make it through the airlock and out the front gate. Freedom was so close Azure could taste it, but she remained cautious, walking on the tips of her bare toes.

Their light steps slowed to a crawl as Ocevia raised her finger to her lips in a silent gesture and peered into the foyer. It all felt too good to be true. Aside from the unconscious guard in front of her cell, they hadn't come across another person.

"There's one guard standing between us and the exit. We're going to have to take him out."

There it was, the other foot. Ocevia was right, but Azure couldn't do it. She was starved, injured, and half-crazed from lack of sleep and an excess of being tortured. The fact that she managed to walk for as long as she had was a miracle.

The blond didn't wait for a response, silently grabbing a large decorative vase from a table beside their hiding place, before making her way toward the unsuspecting male. Corileia, with more confidence than Azure felt, reached for a fireplace poker as she passed and followed the other mermaid.

Azure crept behind them, hoping the guard didn't have the sudden urge to turn around. He was the only thing separating her from open water, from freedom, and, most importantly, from Elios. *Her life-mate.*

Ocevia drew back and swung the large vase hard, smashing it over the guard's skull. His head split open on contact, and he hit the ground almost as fast as the shattered pieces of pottery. Azure still couldn't shake the feeling that their escape had been too easy, but it was too late to go back now. She needed to get Elios as far into the human lands as possible before Miris got her hands on him. Her friend pulled her into the airlock, the healer slipping in behind them, and pressed the button to activate it.

The three mermaids shifted into their true forms as a metal door sealed the small compartment from the palace, and another door slowly opened in front of them, the saltwater flowing steadily into the space. As soon as the metal seal opened enough for them to squeeze out, Ocevia darted for the surface, the others close behind.

Azure's barely healed injuries and weakened state meant nothing as adrenaline propelled her forward. Swimming faster than she thought possible, she still strained to keep up with the others. Their head start would not last. As soon as one of the unconscious guards stirred or they were spotted, the chase would be on. They needed to reach the shore before it was too late.

The sea never felt deeper than it did as they fought their way to the open air, and the rays of sunlight that penetrated the water didn't get closer no matter how much she swam. The distance felt even greater as the first of their pursuers entered Azure's peripheral vision.

Miris' underlings weren't close, but a quick glance over her boney shoulder told her they were gaining on them. There was no way the trio could reach the surface, climb into the boats, and flee before the guards caught up with them.

As they continued their mad dash, the current changed directions unnaturally and caught their tails, yanking them toward to the seafloor. It was too late. Miris knew she'd escaped. She knew, and she was angry. Azure focused her eyes on the surface and forced her body to propel her forward, fear for the man she loved greater than her lack of strength. She needed to reach Elios before the guards did, before the goddess did.

The others swam alongside her, but Ocevia reached out, grasping Azure's wrist and tugging to get her attention. There was no time to waste, and Azure tried to pull her along, but the blond stopped moving and tugged on her again.

She turned to look at her friend, eyes wide with fear and frustration, as the current blasted them from above, pushing them back toward their pursuers. Ocevia smiled and blew Azure a kiss.

Azure's heart stopped as her best friend nodded and pointed at the surface before turning around. Ocevia swam with the current, heading straight for the undersea palace, and the dozen guards chasing them. With a sad smile, Corileia followed. A silent scream escaped her as she watched her friends disappear into the depths.

As much as she wanted to turn around and help Ocevia and the healer, she couldn't. Her friend had made herself clear. She sacrificed herself to stall Miris and the guards so Azure could save their men. With one final heartbreaking glance back, Azure set her jaw in determination and moved her tail as fast as she could, shooting like an arrow at the surface.

Two wooden hulls served as a guiding light as Azure shot upward, and a fresh rush of adrenaline surged through her, closing the distance between her and the men. Her tail shifted to legs just before her face breached the surface.

Elios and Markos each manned the oars of sailboats, idling above Miris' lair. The nonexistent wind would not help in their escape. She gripped the side of Elios' small vessel, but before she could haul herself up, he grabbed her arms and pulled her inside. His mouth descended on hers, and she wasn't sure if the salt she tasted came from the sea, her tears, or his. Feeling his soft lips again was like a slice of paradise, but she pulled away quickly. There was no time for a reunion.

"We have to go. Now!" Her frantic words sounded shrill even to her own ears. They didn't know, couldn't comprehend, the danger they were in. Elios ignored her as he checked her for injuries, and his jaw clenched as he saw her fresh scars, eyes blazing with rage.

"Where's Ocevia?" Markos snapped, fear apparent in his expression. Elios was too distracted with her well-being, but the other man seemed to notice her panicked state.

Azure faced him, her heart shattering further with every syllable.

"We were being chased." Visions of her best friend heading straight for the armed guards made her eyes burn, a knot forming in her throat. She swallowed hard. "She told me to keep going, and then sh-she turned back to stall the guards."

Scanning the water desperately for any sign of Ocevia, Markos' hands slid down his face, and he aged in an instant, horror and grief weighing him down as he slumped in his seat. Azure wanted to go back for her friend, but she needed to get them to safety first.

Movement beneath the water made her heart stutter, and her voice came out with a harsh shriek. "Miris is coming for you! We need to go!"

Elios shook his head, a muscle in his jaw twitching. She'd never seen him look so angry, so determined. "No. We're not leaving without Ocevia."

Water splashed into the boat as several heads broke the surface, none of them blond. She gripped the side of the craft, preparing to jump back into the sea to buy the men some time to escape.

Before she could dive in, a giant figure rose from the depths. The massive body upset the water, and the boats rocked violently, threatening to capsize. Elios held onto the sides, pinning Azure to the wood with his body as waves continued to throw them about.

Tentacles, eight giant tentacles, spread out across the water, grasping the guards that surfaced and yanking them back under. The mermen barely had a chance to scream before their cries were swallowed by the sea.

Azure and her two companions stared in stunned silence as the water leveled out and their boats stilled, as though the Kraken had never burst from the dark depths at all. The appearance of the creature only made her desire to return for her friend stronger. Was Ocevia injured? Had the Kraken wrapped an impossibly large tentacle around her too? The terrifying possibilities were endless.

The water looked like glass. Everything was too still, too quiet. Afraid to draw the sea monster's attention, their boats remained stationary, their oars not daring to delve into the water.

They stared at the calm surface, both men with swords drawn as they waited for something—anything—to happen. Just when Azure thought it might be safe to start rowing toward land, chaos reigned again.

Dark hair was all she could make out as a body shot out of the water at an alarming speed. Azure jumped back, nearly knocking Elios from the boat, as she met the cruel silver stare. Her heart hammered, and the fear she felt from Miris' arrival was so all-consuming that it took her a moment to understand what she was seeing.

A giant tentacle was wrapped around the Sea Goddess's waist, restraining her in the air. The Kraken had Miris.

"Fuck." Markos' voice was low and raspy as he paddled over quickly, bumping up against their boat. Miris thrashed in the Kraken's hold, fighting to break free, but she was only wearing herself out like Azure had when she'd tried to break free from the chains in her underwater prison.

The tentacle tightened, more of its length encircling the goddess as it held her high above the sea. Her hands, the hands that wielded unspeakable magic, were pinned to her sides, rendering her power useless.

The massive octopus-like creature rose slowly from the water. Its rust-colored tentacles proceeding a massive head with a dozen feelers coming from its snout and eyes... the eyes she knew so well. The color was common in her world, but it was the gentle soul behind them she recognized. Azure's hand went to her mouth as she gasped.

"Call off your dog, Azure!" Miris screeched, Elios and Markos turning to her, confusion and surprise coloring their faces. She couldn't speak, her body trembling at the tremendous revelation. "Or my guards *will* destroy every one of you! You think my promises before were scary, little mermaid? I'll make you beg for them before I'm through with you. You want to die fast? Call her off."

The Kraken, clearly displeased with Miris' threats, slammed the goddess into the water violently. Blood dripped from her nose and eyebrow as she was lifted back up, the velocity and height at which she crashed causing damage on impact. She spat, struggling against the tentacled hold, before she stilled.

Her face split into a horrifying grin as her silver eyes stared behind their boats. Azure whipped around, scared of whatever had made the evil goddess so happy, and the sight brought her to her knees.

CHAPTER TWENTY-SEVEN
THE NEW SEA GODDESS

Markos' eyes were wide, unblinking, as a blade pressed firmly against his throat, blood already sliding down his neck from a shallow cut. A malicious grin spread across Lucia's face, one hand covering his mouth while the other gripped her dagger. She looked deranged as her stare locked onto the Kraken's.

Elios shifted on his feet as his knuckles turned white around the hilt of his sword. No one moved, and silence fell, as everyone watched the evil mermaid and her human hostage.

A screeching wail pierced the air, and Azure's eardrums rang painfully. The heart wrenching sound the sea creature made was filled with terror, and its tentacles stopped moving. The Kraken was so still it could have been a giant, terrifying statue.

The creature's eyes never left Markos as the snarling mermaid pushed the blade deeper into his throat. They were at an impasse, but Miris, ever impatient, made the first move.

The Sea Goddess threw her head back and let out an insane cackle before she shouted. "Kill him!"

Lucia's eyes gleamed, her smile impossibly wide as she happily followed the order. Everything happened at once. Her dagger sliced through Markos' throat with no effort before she kicked him overboard, laughing as his body hit the water.

Azure screamed, and Elios threw his sword aside and dove in after his friend. She didn't have time to think, only react, as Lucia focused on her lover.

Snatching Elios' discarded weapon, Azure held the hilt with both hands and swung. The blade sung as it arced through the air. All the time and attention he'd spent tending to the blade showed as its sharp edge split Lucia's abdomen open with little resistance, the mermaid dropping with a thud.

All the while, the Kraken let out a devastated cry that slowly morphed into a scream of rage. More tentacles shot out of the water. With a roar that surely reached the human lands, the Kraken pulled its tentacles in different directions, and with them went pieces of the Sea Goddess.

The silver eyes that had haunted Azure went flying behind the creature, along with the detached head that held them. Each limb shot in a different direction, Miris' torso thrown so far

Azure didn't see where it hit the water. The Sea Goddess was no more. *Miris was dead.*

There was no time for relief. The Kraken dove under the sea, moving toward the spot where Markos' body had gone under. Breaking the surface, Elios gulped for air before submerging once more. Azure jumped overboard to help, her legs turning into a tail before she'd hit the water. For once, she was glad to be a mermaid. Later, after they were far from the sea, she would have time to reflect on what being able to shift after Miris' demise meant for her future, but for that moment, she had to save Elios and recover their friend's body.

The Kraken was already heading for the surface as Azure entered the water, Markos cradled gently in its tentacles. Azure headed for Elios, pulling him up for air, and helping him to their boat as the creature placed the injured man inside. The other boat drifted beside it, bumping gently into theirs as it held Lucia's lifeless body. The creature swatted at the craft, causing it to surge away and capsize, the deceased mermaid reunited with the sea where she'd claimed so many victims.

The Kraken disappeared beneath the water as Azure and Elios climbed into the boat beside Markos. Ocevia's lover was bleeding out too fast, but he was still alive. The choking gasps of his death rattle filled the air, and even as Elios applied pressure to the wound, Azure knew it wouldn't be enough. *Markos would die.*

Azure turned away, not wanting to watch the light in their friend's eyes go out. She had already seen too much death, had wielded too much death. Placing a comforting palm on Elios' back, she stared at the spot where the Kraken had vanished, waiting for something to happen. As though an answer to a question, the familiar blond hair bobbed next to the boat for only a moment before Ocevia heaved herself inside, dropping beside the man she loved. Her heartbroken sobs brought tears to Azure's eyes, and she could barely bring herself to watch as her friend clung to Markos, Ocevia's hands trembling violently.

For a few moments, the only sounds were Ocevia's sobs, and Markos' struggle to survive. As though Ocevia's touch soothed him, the choking gurgle coming from the injured man quieted. Azure closed her eyes, tears streaming down her face. It was her fault. Her best friend had stayed behind, fought off a dozen attackers, trusting her to get the men to safety, and she had failed.

Elios' hand on her thigh pulled her from her thoughts, willing her to open her eyes. For a second, she was convinced none of what she was experiencing was real. Surely, she was back in her cell, experiencing another one of her delusions. When she glanced back at Markos, blood still stained the man's throat, as well as his lover's hands, but the wound was gone. Blinking slowly, he cupped the back of Ocevia's head, pulling her toward him.

"Don't cry, beautiful." His voice was quiet and Ocevia pulled away, disbelief in her eyes as she looked at the now healed man.

"I don't understand." Ocevia's voice shook with emotion, and she kissed Markos hard, tears still falling. Azure's mind whirled as she tried to understand how his wound had healed so quickly, piecing together everything that had happened.

Watching as her friend smoothed Markos' wet hair out of his face, Ocevia's eyes locked on hers.

"Ocevia?" Fear and disbelief paralyzing her, Azure's voice was deathly calm. Her friend didn't respond right away, caressing her lover's face as though to delay the conversation that needed to happen.

"Hmm?" Ocevia's eyes never left Markos' face as she responded, staring at him as though he were a miracle personified. The wound on his neck was completely healed, not so much as a scratch remaining as though it had never happened. Elios sent Azure a questioning glance, but she ignored it as she studied her best friend's face. Both she and Ocevia knew why Markos was healed, but she wanted her friend to say it. Part of her couldn't accept what it meant.

"Ocevia, you killed Miris." Stiffening at the statement, Ocevia sighed before finally meeting Azure's stare.

"I've wanted to tell you for a long time." Ocevia murmured, her voice small. "When I was a child, I couldn't control my powers. I hurt people, Azure, many people. My family..." Her eyes dropped as she reached for the shell necklace at her throat. "I became a mermaid because it was better than being who I was. My family shunned me... they were afraid of me. I didn't tell you because I didn't want you to fear me, too. I couldn't handle you being afraid of me. You were my only friend."

Sorrow filled Azure as she swallowed the lump in her throat. She couldn't imagine the loneliness her best friend had felt, how it must have been to keep such a secret. "I wouldn't abandon you, Ocevia, and I certainly wouldn't fear you." Smiling, she placed her hand on her friend's shoulder, squeezing gently, trying to lighten the mood. "Actually, your Kraken form almost scared my tail off, but if I had known it was you, I wouldn't have batted an eye."

Ocevia let out a surprised giggle as she turned back to Markos'.

Once her friend was smiling, Azure asked about Corileia. In all the chaos, she hadn't seen the redheaded mermaid reappear.

"A guard captured her and took her back to the palace. I was going to go after them, but then I saw Miris heading for the surface and..." She trailed off as she gazed down at her lover. "I couldn't know for sure that you wouldn't shun me if you knew, Azure. My own family feared me. I needed you to leave so I could transform. It was the only way I could protect all of you." Azure watched as her friend wiped away a tear, guilt washing over her.

Markos reached up and passed his thumb across Ocevia's cheek, smoothing away the moisture. "Are you okay?" he asked. His eyes held the warmth of genuine love, and Azure's heart swelled with joy for her best friend. Ocevia needed love, deserved love. Wrapping his fingers around Azure's hand, Elios stroked her knuckles as they watched their friends share the emotional moment.

Ocevia's mouth tipped up in a small smile as she nodded. "All that matters is that you're alive, Markos. That everyone is alive."

Shifting awkwardly, Azure knew someone needed to address Markos' miraculous healing. There were still things unsaid. "Ocevia... You killed Miris. That means—"

"I know what it means," The blonde cut her off, her tone resigned.

Alarm flashed across Markos' features as he tipped Ocevia's face toward him with his hand. "What does it mean, Ocevia? What's going on?"

Leaning into the hand that cradled her, Ocevia closed her eyes, another tear sliding down her cheek. "It means I'm the new Sea Goddess."

CHAPTER TWENTY-EIGHT
EPILOGUE
3 Months Later

"**D**o you miss it?" Elios walked up behind Azure, wrapping his arms around her. She hadn't noticed how long she'd been standing on the balcony, staring out at the sea. The answer to his question was complicated. One of her shoulders lifted in a shrug.

"I don't miss the curse, but I do miss Ocevia." Just thinking about her best friend being forced into the role as the new Sea Goddess reopened the fresh wound in her heart.

She closed her eyes as Elios placed a warm kiss on her cheek. The feel of him holding her filled her with a sense of peace. There was a time in that dark, cold cell where she'd thought she would never see him again. Now she had him forever. "We'll visit soon. I know you must miss her dearly. I miss Markos too."

Before Azure left the sea on that fateful day, Ocevia had used the powers she'd inherited from Miris to release her from her bargain. Azure's tail was gone forever, something that made her unexpectedly sad, but so was her duty to kill. She would be able to live the rest of her human life with Elios, no longer having to run for their lives. It was an act that Azure could never repay, and something Ocevia could never do for herself.

Reaching around her, Elios touched the sapphire engagement ring on her finger. The stone glittered in the sun, catching the brilliant rays and reflecting them into the air. "We should head out soon."

Azure nodded and gazed up at her fiancé, drinking in every detail of his handsome face. "I'm a little scared. It's been so long. What if she doesn't want to live with us in Starspell?"

A smile spread across Elios' now clean-shaven face. "I'm sure Daneliya is nervous, too. And if she doesn't want to live with us, we can just move to Thatia. We're free to live wherever we want."

Freedom was something she'd never expected to have again, and she didn't know what to do with it. She smiled up at him and experienced an epiphany. The sea was no longer her home, but as she stared into his ocean-blue eyes, she knew she would always see it in his loving gaze.

Her fractured heart was almost whole. The song of death would never fall from her lips again, and her family was about to be reunited. For the first time in her life, Azure was excited to see what the future held.

"You're right. Let us go. It's been over three years. I don't want to keep my little sister waiting."

THE END

Azure's story may be coming to a close... for now... but Ocevia's story is next!

ENJOYED SONG OF DEATH?

If you enjoyed this book, don't forget to leave a review!

Reviews are vital to authors! They help books reach new readers. I really appreciate it!

Leave a review here:
https://www.amazon.com/Song-Death-Supernatural-Saviors-Book-ebook/dp/B0B141CMF1

Sign up for C. A. Varian's newsletter to receive current updates on her new and upcoming releases, sales, and giveaways:
https://sendfox.com/cavarian

You can also find all stories, books, and social media pages and follow her here:
https://linktr.ee/cavarian
https://cavarian.com/

Also By

Hazel Watson Mystery Series
Kindred Spirits: Prequel
The Sapphire Necklace
Justice for the Slain
Whispers from the Swamp
Crossroads of Death
The Spirit Collector

Crown of the Phoenix Series
Crown of the Phoenix
Crown of the Exiled
Crown of the Prophecy (Coming May 2024)
Mate of the Phoenix
Shadowed by Prophecy
Shadowed by the Veil (Coming Soon)

Supernatural Savior Series
Song of Death
Goddess of Death

An Other World Series
The Other World
The Other Key
The Other Fate

My Alien Mate Series
My Alien Protector

Survivor & Savior Duet
Saving Scarlett
Keeping Caroline (Coming July 2024)

Second Chance with Santa

Born of Fire

ACKNOWLEDGEMENTS

I want to thank my editor, Megan, of Willow Oak Author services, for putting up with my crazy editing schedule. (At least I keep the work coming).

I would like to thank Leigh Cadiente of Leigh Cover Designs for this book's amazing cover.

Thank you to Breezy Jones for the amazing art and for being my new BFF. We should probably talk a little bit less at 3am though. I'm tired.

Thank you to my PA, Jasmine. I'm so grateful for all you do to help me! I am the single most unorganized person in the world, so I don't know what I would do without you. You may need to make a list of what I need you to do for me, because I can't remember what I'm forgetting.

Thank you to Charlee, of Blurbs, Baubles, and Book Covers, for making my world maps for this series. I miss you, girl!

Thank you so much to my phenomenal Street Team, Mikela Jones, Laura Farrell, Sierra Crawford, Amber Gamble, Jule Hayes, LeeRenee Musgjerd, Pyro Ember, Tasha Melton, Samantha Gentry, Chelsea Savage, Halley Peagler, Jeanann Leary, Illisa Lea, Michele Vaughan, Jessica Spain, Debbie Webb, Autumn Gresser-Chambers, Nichole Crawley, Yvonne Aguilera, Lauren Landry, Karina Serrano, Kerrie Porter, Natali Garcia, Molly Mazure, Destiny Del Palacio, Yesenia Rosado, and a few others! You guys are so good to me!

Thank you so much to Teena Scott for an amazing audiobook performance! (and for being a great friend).

My final thank you is to my family, friends, and most of all, my readers.

Thank you for your support!

ABOUT THE AUTHOR

Raised in a small town in the heart of Louisiana's Cajun Country, C. A. Varian spent most of her childhood fishing, crabbing, and getting sunburnt at the beach. Her love of reading began very young, and she would often participate in school reading challenges.

Graduating with the first of her college degrees as a mother of two in her late twenties, she became a public-school teacher, teaching for twelve years, both social studies and special education. As of the release of this book, she was finally able to resign from teaching to write full time!

Writing became a passion project, and she put out her first novel in 2021. She has continued to publish new novels every few months since then, not slowing down for even a minute.

Married to a retired military officer, she spent many years moving around for his career, but they currently live in central Alabama, along with her youngest daughter, Arianna. Her oldest daughter, Brianna, is enjoying her happily ever after with her new husband and several pups. C.A. Varian has two Shih Tzus that she considers her children. Boy, Charlie, and girl, Luna, are their mommy's shadows. She also has three cats named Ramses, Simba, and Cookie.

Made in the USA
Las Vegas, NV
07 November 2024

11245313R00201